SOFT TARGET

MCU BOOK 1

IAIN ROB WRIGHT

ULCERATED PRESS

WANT FREE BOOKS?

Don't miss out on your FREE Iain Rob Wright starter pack. Five bestselling horror novels sent straight to your inbox for FREE. No strings attached.

FULL INFO AT BACK OF BOOK

Dedicated with those with scars.

With Thanks to:

Sean Ellis
&
Chris Kirk

Everything I got right, I got right because of them.

"Great Britain has lost an empire but has not yet found a role."

– Dean Acheson

"Terrorism has no nationality or religion."

– Vladamir Putin

"Damn it!"

– Jack Bauer, 24, Fox Network Television

1

PROLOGUE

Birds flocked over the town square as young and old alike scoffed popcorn and candyfloss. Their shuffling bottoms filled every bench, and an exuberant rock band assaulted their eardrums. Those who could find no seats stood and lifted their plastic beer cups along to the music. Stretched between a pair of gnarled oak trees, a banner painted with bright red letters declared: **MAY 25th SPRING FETE: Getting nutty in Knutsford.**

Carnival games and food stalls had sprung up everywhere in the last twenty-four hours, their operators as ruthlessly efficient as a German car factory. Jeffrey Blanchfield stood beneath the sagging blue-and-white bunting and gazed up at the azure sky. Crisp and pure, the springtime air was overpowered by the wafting scent of fresh-cut grass, and the cooing of pigeons signalled the start of a lovely afternoon. Behind one single cloud, the bright sun blazed.

Fresh air was something Jeffrey enjoyed, ever since his childhood on granddaddy's farm. He'd tried to take Margaret to see the old place once—on their fourth anniversary—but the parcel of land where it stood had been paved to make way for a trading estate. He hadn't realised at the time, but a part of him had died the day he realised that old farm had gone. As a boy he'd often stood amongst the cows, breathing in the heady aromas of country air and fresh dung. Nowadays, thirty-five million cars had fouled the country air and the cow dung had been replaced by paved minefields of dog shit.

Jeffrey's worn kneecaps clicked and yelled. He let out a shiver. Even today in the bright sunshine he wore his long grey anorak.

When had he got so old?

Ahead, a young girl with sapphire ribbons tied in her pigtails and a stuffed bear tucked under one arm held a mongrel on a lead. She was alone, and watching the fete with curious interest as her scruffy pet cocked its leg over a flowerbed. Jeffrey knew it was wrong to approach the girl, but he always found young ones so insightful. Their opinions were indicative of the current state of society, and he wanted to know where things currently stood. He wanted to make sure, one last time, that what he was doing was right.

He and Margaret had never managed children—Jeffrey's fault, thanks to a low sperm count—and perhaps if they'd been able to make a family, things would have turned out different.

Jeffrey would have made a great father.

He approached the young girl, moving close enough to pick up her scent. His hairy nostrils detected mummy's perfume mixed with sugary sweets: the smells of childhood mixed with an impatience to grow up. Jeffrey wondered if he'd ever tried to wear his father's aftershave as a child, but couldn't remember. It was so hard to remember anything these days.

The little girl turned and noticed Jeffrey standing over her. "Hello," she said warily.

"Hello, there. How are you doing today, young lady? Enjoying the fete?"

"I won a teddy bear," she pointed to a badly-stitched gypsy prize tucked beneath her arm. "On the darts game over by the duck pond."

"How splendid!" Jeffrey knelt to pat the girl's mongrel on the head. It was some kind of diluted beagle, a half-breed like most the world nowadays. "And what is this little fella's name?"

"Ruby. She's a girl."

"Ruby? What a pretty name."

"I called her it 'cus it's my favourite stone. When I get married, I'm gunna have a big ruby on my weddin' finger." She raised her hand and wiggled her ring finger at him.

"Don't you dream of doing something other than getting married and having an expensive ring? Don't you want to do anything special?"

Jeffrey's voice had unwittingly taken on a disapproving tone which obviously upset the girl. "I... I'd like to be a vet and help animals. I like animals."

Jeffrey nodded, then reached down and patted the girl's head. "Now, that's a good profession, young lady. Your mummy and daddy will be very proud."

"I don't have a daddy."

Jeffrey sighed. "Another careless pregnancy, no doubt. So many of them nowadays. Women today have such little self-respect, and men no better—work-shy hoodlums and ignorant bastards, the lot of them." He realized his lack of manners and covered his mouth with a withered old hand. "Forgive my language, young lady. The internal filters start to go at my age."

"You said a bad word. Mummy!" She scanned the crowd, yanking at the poor mongrel's neck. A heavyset woman emerged from the crowd grasping a beaker full of cider in one hand and a dripping grease burger in the other. Her flabby breasts spilled from an undersized halter-top, and she sported a ghastly tattoo of a flower on her flabby right foot.

"Was up, bab?" the woman asked in a thick 'brummie' accent. "Was wrung?"

Ugly way of talking, Jeffrey thought to himself. *If ever there was a region so proud of sounding stupid, it's Birmingham.*

Jeffrey had visited Smethwick once for a football match a colleague invited him to. Never again. It had been a dirty, grimy, uncivilised place, full of people spitting and snarling. There had been a pub by the stadium with boarded-up windows and peeling blue paint. The North was a much nicer region of the country in general, but even that was going downhill fast.

The little girl pointed an accusing finger at Jeffrey. "He said a bad word, mummy."

The fat mother glared at Jeffrey, narrowing her heavily made-up eyes. Jeffrey hid his disdain of the woman behind a polite smile. "My mistake, Ma'am, I promise you. Your sweet daughter has already had an apology from me, but I offer one to you too. Forgive my manners. Mind wobbles at my age, I'm afraid."

The woman wrapped a chubby arm around her daughter. "Nay problem." But as she moved away she muttered something else: "Dirty old perv."

Jeffrey rolled his eyes. You couldn't hold a conversation these days without somebody accusing you of something. Because most people were indeed up to something. Jeffrey was usually the exception, but today even he had sins to commit.

Nearby, a teenage girl writhed up against an older boy, a group of lads leering at the bright pink thong peeking out the back of her jeans. Nobody took exception to the lewd display—the sight of flesh-on-flesh and tongue-in-mouth was something younger generations took no offence to. Things that had once been private and intimate—respectful—were now frivolous and undervalued. Jeffrey sighed and wondered where it would end. Would people rut in the street fifty years from now? Would they start taking animals into their beds?

Jeffrey remembered the green and pleasant land of his childhood and missed it dearly. He remembered when a foreigner was a novelty instead of a sucking parasite or a potential criminal. He remembered when women, like his beloved Margaret, possessed self-respect, and men knew what hard work was. Remembered when children were seen and not heard.

It had all turned to shit. Jeffrey had seen more of this life than he'd ever intended to. It had made him sick. He pushed his way through the crowd, receiving a drenched elbow from a carelessly held cup of cider for his troubles. He winced and frowned as cuss words flew over his head like fluttering sparrows. Exposed cleavages sullied the scenery along with great puddles of alcohol and half-eaten food. All around, people danced in their own tawdry filth.

Jeffrey made his way to the bandstand, suffering the glancing blows, drunken shoves, and reckless swearing with gritted teeth. He was Jesus walking the *Via Dolorosa,* disregarded and misunderstood, but history would show that he was the righteous one. It was everybody else who was damned. Jeffrey's sacrifice would be remembered and what he did today would improve future generations by making them see what was truly important.

By the time Jeffrey reached the bandstand, his arthritic knees were hot coals and his ribs stung from a dozen elbow digs. The tribute band had just finished their latest number and were now interacting with the crowd. "Who's enjoying themselves?" the lead singer crowed.

The audience cheered. Beer and cider flew from their cups and spattered the ground, a dirty baptism of cigarette ash and alcohol.

"Is everybody ready for a rocking summer?"

More cheers.

"Now, before we play our next number, me and the band would just like to thank you for being such a wicked audience."

'Wicked' is the correct word, thought Jeffrey.

"You people really know how to have a good time."

In case Jeffrey had any doubts about what he was going to do, he studied the crowd one last time and reminded himself of the reasons he was there. He spotted a group of people his own age gyrating and snogging like teenaged lovers. It was sickening. His hatred had led him there, but all he felt now was pity—pity for these deluded souls.

Jeffrey's mission had begun the moment his beloved Margaret died at his feet clutching her chest and pleading for life not to leave her. But it had left her. There had been nothing he could do for her but watch her die on the worn carpet of their cold living room.

The heart attack had been inevitable as soon as the government began housing benefit seekers and minorities in the houses next to theirs. He and Margaret had broken their backs working to pay-off the mortgage on their humble three-bed semi, worked their whole lives so they could enjoy a retirement together. But when their twilight years finally arrived, they were filled with stress and aggravation. Petty crime had taken over the town—theft and vandalism on every corner. Margaret became afraid to leave the house, unwilling to risk the haranguing of the local youths congregating in every underpass. The constant fear and worrying had eventually taken her from Jeffrey by bursting her heart. She'd been too gentle to cope, his dear Margaret. That was why she'd gone on to a better place while Jeffrey was stuck in the cesspit that had become the United Kingdom.

United, huh? I've never known people to be so selfish.

When someone had given Jeffrey an opportunity to change things, he hadn't needed to think twice. He'd accepted the mission willingly, eagerly, and was now finally ready to follow through with it. His actions would set something magnificent in motion. The opening act of a grand scheme designed to make the world take a long, hard look at itself. Only then would people change. Only then will kind souls like his Margaret no longer be preyed upon.

Jeffrey took the first step towards the bandstand.

The lead singer noticed him. "Hey up, we've got a new member of the band. You lost, old fella?"

Jeffrey ignored the singer and carried on up the steps.

This amused the singer more. "Here, looks like he's coming to sing one with us. Do we all want to see the old fella sing?" The crowd cheered. "I'm not sure we have anything by George Formby, though. How about *When I'm Sixty-Four?*"

The crowd bellowed with laughter.

Jeffrey made his way up the last steps, taking advantage of the band's confusion. He was able to stroll right up to the mic stand where he proceeded to say what he had come there to say. "You people disgust me."

Jeffrey pulled open his anorak and detonated the bomb strapped around his waist.

2

FALLING DOWN

Summer was nearly here, but the bugs were early. Sarah hopped from the bus to the sticky pavement and swatted at a wasp. When the buzzing menace refused to flee, she gritted her teeth and snarled, but the wasp seemed amused by her frustration. As it dove at her head for a third time, Sarah's temper flared, and she snatched it out of the air and crushed it in her fist. The dickish creature got off a parting shot before it died, and the piercing pain in Sarah's palm reminded her of the virtue of calm. Getting angry only ever hurt her, yet it was her default emotion—the one she always grasped at first. Often as not, it would be followed by guilt, which is what she felt now for having taken the life of something weaker than her.

She threw the crushed wasp carcass to the pavement and resumed her journey. *Sorry, Mr Wasp, but you picked the wrong woman to mess with. You were the one who made it personal.*

As she marched through the high street, Sarah could have ignored the gawking strangers glancing at her scars, but instead, she met their stares head-on. If they wanted to gawp, she had every right to stare right back at them. Either that or they could pay for the freak show.

It didn't take long to reach the bank. It was in the middle of Birmingham's busy Corporation Street. Sarah joined the winding queue inside and grunted. Out of the six serving windows, just two were manned. She glanced at the gaping arse-crack of the woman queuing in front of her, and at the snot-nosed toddler running around screaming, and sighed.

The toddler stopped its screaming for a second when it spotted Sarah's disfigured face. Sarah bared her teeth, and the child hurried away. Its mother was too busy with her iPhone to give a shit. Sarah often wondered why people had children when they couldn't be bothered to watch them.

If Sarah could've helped it, she'd do away with her monthly trips to the bank. Other aspects of her life could be dealt with via the Internet or over the phone, but there was no choice when it came to the bank. She needed to visit the city once a month to pay in her foreign cheques for US dollars.

"Come on," she mumbled as the queue moved by a single body. Her wasp sting was itching now. She ran her ragged nails over her throbbing palm and tried to ease it. She regretted crushing the wasp. They were alike. People flinched at the sight of Sarah, too.

A well-kempt businessman strolled away from the tellers after having concluded his business. He smiled at Sarah as he approached, but once he got close enough to see the far side of her face, his eyes fixed on the floor and he sped up.

Men often gave Sarah a smile if they caught her good side—from that angle she was a shapely blonde woman—but as soon as they glimpsed the scarred left side of her face, their stomachs turned and they'd act as if they suddenly realised they were in a hurry. It happened so often that Sarah didn't even care anymore

The queue inched forward. Sarah shuffled along. It was Monday morning, didn't the bank expect to have so many customers? What made things worse was that there were another three members of staff available, but they were hanging around in an office behind the serving windows. One guy was even swigging coffee and laughing, oblivious to the customers waiting.

Sarah thought about the bomb that had gone off yesterday in the town of Knutsford. Were all those people hanging around like this, thinking everything was normal? Did they even see it coming?

She'd visited Knutsford once. A place just outside Manchester with a cosy Italian restaurant that served the best ravioli she'd ever tasted. She and her husband, Thomas, had eaten there one night before they caught a flight out from Manchester Airport. Thomas had ordered spaghetti and made her leak wine out of her nose by letting the strands hang out of his mouth like a monster. Knutsford was a nice place. Sarah had been shocked to see it littered with bodies on last night's evening news.

The BBC claimed some disgruntled pensioner was behind the attack, but that just raised more questions than it answered. Like: how did a retired postal worker learn how to make a nail bomb? And why attack a town like Knutsford?

The queue shuffled up another half-step. Four of the six serving windows were still unoccupied. The dickhead in the office was still sipping coffee and laughing, while his equally lazy colleagues joined him in ignoring the bank's waiting customers.

Sarah had suffered enough. She exited the queue and marched on up to the serving window. "Hey, d'you think you might come out and do your jobs for a while?" she shouted through the security glass. "There are people waiting out here, in case you hadn't noticed."

A few chuckles from the people standing in the queue, but mostly awkward silence. The young guy with the coffee ambled towards the other side of the window like a swaggering cowboy. He was wearing a cheap suit with garish cufflinks he clearly thought were stylish. His badge read: 'Assisant Branch Manager'. Sarah wondered if he was aware of the spelling mistake. She guessed not. When he noticed the scars on Sarah's face, he stumbled mid-step, but recovered well enough to make it to the window and pretend he hadn't noticed. "Ma'am, you need to join the queue."

"I *did* join the queue, but I'm worried that by the time you people get to me, I will have joined the afterlife."

"Ma'am, if you won't join the queue and wait to be served, I will have to ask you to leave."

"And I will have to ask you to kiss my arse. All these people are waiting while you're standing around like a couple of monkeys."

The Assisant Branch Manager adjusted his tie and looked down his nose at her. "I'm now asking you to leave, ma'am."

Sarah folded her arms. "So you won't let me cash the cheque I get from the US Army for my dead husband? He was blown up in Afghanistan, in case you're wondering. It was so bad they couldn't even put his body back together. And what about the money I get from the British government for losing half my face fighting for this country? Will you not help me with that? Look, I understand you like to drink your cappuccino in the back and pretend you're a real businessman, but I need my money to live. I'm strange like that."

The *Assisant* Branch Manager shifted uncomfortably. "I'm... very sorry to hear that, ma'am, but I'm afraid you'll need to leave if you're going to be difficult. Please call our customer service number if you'd like to make a complaint."

Sarah moved her face right up to the glass so that the obstinate prick could get a good look at her. "I'm not the one being difficult. Don't you people get paid enough not to treat your customers like a nuisance? Your job is to serve us, but you make it seem like you're doing us a favour. We give you our money and you act like it's yours. We ask for it back and you make us jump through hoops. You fine and charge us every chance you get, then refuse to explain why, as if we should just accept that you make the rules. Well, let me tell you something, Mr Assisant Manager, I got my face blown off fighting in a foreign country so that oil companies and fat cat bankers like your bosses could keep their big houses and shiny sports cars. So, when I say get your bone-idle arses out here right now and do your goddamn jobs, I think I earned the right to say so."

There was an outright cheer from the queue of customers. They were solidly behind her now, but the *Assisant* Manager was not. He nodded over Sarah's shoulder, as if he were Augustus Caesar having a dissenting peasant dragged away and executed.

Sarah spun around to see a wide-shouldered security guard stomping towards her. With his bald head and tattoos he looked absurd in the smart uniform they'd given him. "You've been asked to leave, luv."

"And yet I'm still here. Whatever should we do?"

More chuckles. The crowd was egging her on, eager to see what happened. Sarah rolled her eyes. They were happy to let a disfigured freak entertain them for a while, but she doubted any of them would step in and help her if she needed it.

"You need to leave," the guard commanded, giving her his best impression of a snarling bear.

Sarah waved a hand in front of her face. "And you need to take a breath mint."

The guard reached out his hand to grab her shoulder.

Without thinking, Sarah grabbed the big man's hand and twisted it. She yanked him one way and then the other, flipping him over his own wrist. It was a basic Aikido throw, and one that was second-nature to her. *Like riding a rusty old bike.*

The guard hit the ground like a sack of potatoes. He was unhurt, but more than a little surprised. Sarah stood over him and snarled. "I'd advise against standing up, mate, or I'll make a deposit up your arse with my foot."

The other customers bellowed with laughter. Their blood lust was up and the violence had excited them. Sarah knew enough about mob mentality to know how people's morals soon changed when their neighbours acted up. It was time to leave; she'd made her point.

Sarah looked back at the stunned Assisant Manager, still safe behind his glass barrier, and pointed her finger at him. "Get your name badge replaced, dickhead. It gives away how much of an idiot you are." She then strolled out of the bank and into the crisp air of early May, wondering how the hell she would get by without her cheques being cashed. Maybe if she came back tomorrow they wouldn't remember her face.

Yeah right!

Sarah picked up her pace and hurried away from the bank. If they called the police she would be easy to identify. Heavily scarred women wearing jeans and work boots were easy to spot, and sure enough, it didn't take long before Sarah was certain she was being followed.

Her pursuer was staying back, slipping behind other pedestrians. Every time Sarah looked back, the man pretended to be busy with his phone or the produce of a nearby market stall. He was wearing the long grey coat of a middle-class car salesman.

Sarah slid into an alleyway between two estate agents and headed around the rear of the high street, where there was only a car park and a dingy hairdresser's. She picked up speed and glanced over her shoulder. The man could make no secret of pursuing her now. His footsteps echoed on the concrete behind her, keeping pace rather than catching up. He was apparently in no rush to catch her.

Sarah rounded a brick wall that sectioned off a small parking yard belonging to the bank, of all places, and slid herself behind a large, steel wheelie bin. Her pursuer would've seen her sneak around the wall and into the parking yard, but wouldn't have seen her slip behind the bin.

The stranger approached, his footsteps growing louder. Sarah crouched and waited.

Clip clop clip clop.

Clip clop.

Clip.

Sarah leapt up from behind the wheelie bin and swung her leg in a flying roundhouse. It was a knockout blow, designed to end the confrontation before it had chance to begin. If the stranger was an off-duty police officer, taking his head off was an ill-advised action, but he asked for it when he'd started with the cloak-and-dagger bullshit.

The stranger ducked Sarah's leg and swept her feet out from under her as soon as she landed. She was so surprised, that her head struck the concrete and left her lying in a daze.

"Captain Stone," said the stranger. "I prefer to shake hands upon meeting, but I'm open to other customs too. Would you like to get up and try something easier?"

Sarah gazed up at the man and saw he was clean-cut and

handsome. His chin jutted like a superhero's and his dark sideburns could have been shaped by a laser. Not a single crease found its way onto the tailored shirt beneath his grey coat.

This guy isn't Old Bill.

Sarah shoved herself backwards and sprang to her feet, then leapt at the man again, this time opting for fists. Her first blow missed, glancing sideways off a blocking forearm, and her follow-up blows struck thin air. Her humiliation was compounded by her legs being swept out from under her again.

As soon as she hit the ground, Sarah sprung up and launched into yet another attack, but this time the man pulled a gun from inside his coat and pointed it at her forehead. "You're testing my patience, Captain Stone," he said. "Please, calm down."

Sarah let her fists drop to her sides, but kept them clenched. "Who the hell are you?" she demanded.

The man let his own fists drop and took a step closer. "You can call me Howard."

Sarah frowned. The man didn't look like a 'Howard.' "What do you want with me?"

"An afternoon of your time."

Sarah went to turn away. "Sorry, I'm busy."

"Busy with what? Cashing the pittance the US Government begrudgingly pays you in widow's benefits, or the marginally more generous giro the British Government gives you for taking half your face?"

Sarah snarled. The mention of her scars made them tingle, and her left eye blinked sorely where the pink creases met her eyelid. "You know nothing."

"I know that you made a fine Captain until you hit that IED, the same day that a British missile mistakenly took your husband, US Army Ranger, Lieutenant Thomas Geller. I know that you've been slinking around for the last five years like a feral fox, snapping at anybody who comes too close. You're angry, Sarah, and I don't blame you."

Sarah snorted. "So what," she said. "Half the world is angry. The other half are pushovers. What do you care?"

Howard looked at her. It had been a long time since any man had kept his eyes on her for more than a few seconds. "I can give you the chance to do some good again, Sarah," he said. "I want to give you the opportunity to pull yourself out of the quagmire of despair you're in."

"Who are you?" Sarah was getting tired of the vague talk and wanted straight answers. "Who do you work for?"

"An agency you've never heard of. An agency whose job it is to keep this country safe. I work for the government."

Sarah smiled. "You work for the government? Well, why didn't you say so? In that case, you can go to Hell."

She tried to walk away again.

"The bomb that went off yesterday..."

Sarah stopped walking and turned back. "Yeah, good job protecting the country there. How many died?"

"Forty-two. The people responsible have owned up to it."

"People? I heard it was a geriatric with a grudge."

"It was," said Howard. "The bomber was Jeffrey Blanchfield. Sixty-eight years of age and a retired postman, just like the news reported, but there's more. The grudge may have been his, but the bomb came from Shab Bekheir."

Sarah froze. For a moment, she couldn't move or speak. She spluttered before she could get her words out. "Y-you're telling me that a terrorist cell in Afghanistan is responsible for a pensioner blowing up a town in Cheshire?" She couldn't help but laugh; it was ridiculous.

Howard was serious. "We received a videotape this

morning taking credit for the attack. Al Al-Sharir made the claim himself."

Sarah's eyes widened. Her scars stretched and itched, the wasp sting on her palm throbbed, and her blood was pulsing. "Al-Sharir?"

"That's right," Howard continued, "Al-Sharir, the man responsible for the IED that hit your squad. You're the only one who survived, right?"

"No one made it out alive that day, not really."

"Fancy a chance at getting even?"

"What? By going with you? I don't even know you."

"No, you don't, but what do you have to lose by trusting me? I didn't go to the trouble of tracking you down just to pull your leg. You have experience we can use Sarah. Help us."

Sarah didn't have to think. The guy was right, what did she have to lose? "Where are we going?"

"A place that doesn't exist."

Sarah was about to ask what he meant when a door opened at the back of the parking yard. A man stepped out of the bank's rear exit. To Sarah's surprise, it was the *Assisant* Manager, out for a cigarette, no doubt while the bank's queue still trailed out the front entrance.

Sarah stretched her neck, and it clicked. She looked at Howard and said, "Just let me deal with something, and I'll be right with you, okay?"

Howard looked confused, but shrugged and nodded.

When the *Assisant* Manager saw Sarah stomping toward him, he seemed at first surprised, then worried. As she got closer, however, he stood his ground, puffing up his chest like a peacock.

Sarah grinned. Men never ran from a woman; they always thought they were the ones with the power.

Sarah kicked the smug git right in the bollocks before walking back to Howard. “Okay,” she said. “Now we can go.”

3

THE GAME

"Where are you parked?" Sarah asked Howard.

"Nearby. My colleague is waiting for us."

"It's not Will Smith, is it?"

"No."

"Pity. I thought you might have been the men in black."

"I'm not wearing black."

"Good point."

Howard kept them to the back streets, heading away from the city centre. It was a part of town Sarah hadn't visited before, and it was none too pretty. The well-kept Victorian buildings of Birmingham's nucleus gradually gave way to rundown terraces, oily tyre-fitting garages, and ethnic food stores. They walked for twenty minutes before Sarah became impatient enough to say something. "Where the hell are you taking me? Maybe you should show me your badge or something before we go any further."

"We're almost there," was all Howard said. Despite the lack of assurances, Sarah's curiosity spurred her on.

When they crossed over a one-way street, to the chagrin of a beeping van driver, Howard said little else. "We couldn't arrive directly in the city centre. We had to touch down on the outskirts."

"Touch down?"

Howard smirked, his default expression, and his hero's chin jutted out every time he did it. "Come on," he said, "just inside here."

Sarah studied an old scrap yard in front of her. The gates were hanging open, but wicked spikes lined the top of the surrounding fence. "Oh, hell no," she said. "You're not getting me in there. This is starting to feel like a mob hit."

"Are you always so dramatic?"

"Look at this face," Sarah pointed to her scars. "I'm the Phantom of the bloody Opera. I can't help being dramatic."

Howard kept his smirk and forged ahead without comment. He passed through the open gates and headed inside the scrap yard. Despite her better judgment, Sarah followed. She hated to admit it, but this was the most stimulated she'd been in years. After avoiding people for so long, Sarah had become involved in some kind of intrigue with a man she'd just met; a man who could take her in a fight. That was intriguing by itself. Sarah might have been rusty, but she was a past practitioner of Aikido, Muy Thai, and Krav Maga. There weren't many people who could put her on her back so easily.

They headed deeper into the scrap yard, passing engineless car frames and machinery carcasses. Nobody else was around, which was weird. With the gates hanging wide open, Sarah expected to see a couple of employees at least.

"Just around here," said Howard. He cut behind a rusty shipping container and disappeared from sight. Sarah slowed, her body tensing. She knew nothing of Howard, and being led into an abandoned scrap yard wasn't exactly comforting, but she had come this far.

Sarah took a deep breath, then sprang around the side of the rusty container, ready to fight at the first sign of danger.

"Hop aboard," said Howard, pointing to an idling helicopter as if it were the most normal thing in the world.

The Griffin HAR2 was painted a solid black instead of its typical earthen hues, and the RAF insignia were missing from its tail boom. Sarah hadn't seen one of the plump, twin-engine helicopters since a training mission in Cyprus ten years ago. Seeing one made her think of the Mediterranean Sea and the feeling of sun and salt on her skin. Of all her memories of the Army, it was one of the few nice ones.

"I'm not getting in that helicopter unless you tell me where we're going."

Howard gave a hand signal to the helicopter pilot and turned to face her. "Sarah, your father is a major in the SAS, is he not?"

Sarah's eyes went wide. "I don't know what you're on about. My father is a major in the Royal Logistics Corp. He's in charge of ordering the regimental bog roll."

Howard chuckled. "I know everything about you, Sarah, so there's no point lying. I know that your father is Major Curtis Stone, and that you are the only female in the history of the British Armed Forces who has taken and passed the SAS selection tests, despite not being accepted afterwards."

Sarah couldn't help but snarl. She'd outperformed and outlasted all the men in the selection tests, but had been denied entry anyway, overtly because of her sex. The only reason they'd even let her try out was because her father had pulled strings. To top it off, her father had only pulled those strings because he'd been so sure she'd fail, giving him yet another reason to belittle her. She showed him though—proved that she was as good as any man—but they turned around and reminded her it didn't matter so long as the world was still controlled by cocks and balls. She'd gone through two weeks of the grimmest hell she could imagine, for nothing. The strength and unwillingness to quit she'd possessed during those gruelling trials had never truly returned to her. Her father had extinguished it the day he told her she had no place in the SAS, and that doubt had followed her for the rest of her career.

Howard folded his arms. "The Government keeps secrets, Sarah. You know that as well as anyone. I cannot give you the location until you've been given the proper clearances. I promise that at the end of a short helicopter ride, all will be revealed. After that, you can choose to help us or not. A quick signature on an Official Secrets document and you can stay or leave at your leisure."

Sarah chewed her bottom lip. She was distrustful of anyone with a Government stamp on their pay cheques, but she had to know what was going on and why Howard knew so much about her. Her natural proclivity was to investigate, and it was very hard to fight against. She needed to find out what was going on.

"Okay," she said, "but you try to stick a blindfold on me and I'll bite your face."

Howard raised an eyebrow. "There won't be any need for that."

And there wasn't. When Sarah stepped into the rear of the helicopter, she found that the windows on both sides blacked out. All she could see was the passenger cabin and the cockpit ahead.

The man behind the controls was a giant. His shoulders were twice the width of the seat and bulged out on either side. His neck was as thick as Sarah's thigh, and his face was almost as ugly as hers.

"This is Mandy," Howard said, getting into the co-pilot's seat.

"Mandy? Isn't that a girl's name?"

"His name is Manny Dobbs," said Howard. "Mandy is just a nickname. Yours will be 'pain-in-the-arse' if you don't start being nicer."

"Scarface would suit me better."

"Bit cliche, don't you think?"

"Oldies are the goodies."

Howard turned back to face the front and exchanged a few quiet words with Mandy. Soon the engine started up and the rotors spun. The gentle rocking gave way to a sudden lurch, and then they were off, airborne.

"The flight will take forty minutes," Howard informed her. "Take a load off and I'll tell you when we're near."

Sarah eased back in her seat. As she glanced around, she noticed that much of the interior differed from the utilitarian RAF model she knew. Nylon rigging and handholds lined the cabin's roof, and additional compartments and cabinets filled the walls. Even the cockpit was sleeker than normal, the stark dashboard replaced by something akin to a modern day 4x4.

Once again Sarah wondered, and worried, who she'd agreed to ride along with. Whoever they were, they were no branch of the Military she knew of. Perhaps they were civvies or some private organisation, but the way Howard had fought her, and the fact he carried a concealed weapon, made her wonder if that could be true either.

All of these thoughts tired her, and the comfort of the chair sucked her inwards, swaddling her like a colicky babe. The vibration of the engine massaged her back. She couldn't help but close her eyes and take a nap.

. . .

AFGHANISTAN, 2008

The heat in Afghanistan was like everything else in Afghanistan: out to kill you. It burned your skin, without you realising it, until you took a shower and gritted your teeth as your whole body screamed.

While parts of the country were green and pleasant, others were nothing but mud and desert, or mountainous rock and shale. When the wind was up, you couldn't open your eyes for fear of getting grit in them. But all that paled in comparison to the people. There was no difference between the civilians who wanted to help and the Taliban who wanted blood. Both looked and dressed the same, and both waved and smiled whenever they saw British soldiers. It was like fighting with shadows—impossible to tell friend from foe.

That was why Sarah was glad she was getting out. She'd entered Sandhurst Military Academy because that was what members of her family did—at least that's what the men did. The Armed Forces were an esteemed tradition in the Stone family, and joining had seemed a good way to impress her father, but it had only horrified him. He had sent her to college to become a lawyer or a vet, not a butch Jane with a rifle she was too dainty to handle. Her father, most of all, would be pleased that she had decided to leave the Army to play homemaker. But she wasn't doing it for him, she was doing it for Thomas.

Sarah met Thomas at Camp Bastion, a British military base the size of Reading. The US Camp Leatherneck adjoined it and their personnel would often come onto British turf to share intel, play sports, or take advantage of the softer alcohol rules. While there was always a 'them and us' mentality between the two camps, there was also a great camaraderie.

Thomas was a Ranger with the 75th, an officer who shared information on a Taliban enclave his squad had surveyed in a surrounding village. He didn't have the forces to handle it himself, and there were no significant US reinforcements in the region. As the village fell under the purview of British patrol routes, Sarah had to hear Thomas out and act on his intel. His offer of sharing a bootleg bottle of wine with her in the Officer's NAAFI that same evening had been above and beyond what was expected, but his wide smile and Floridian drawl had won her over. Eight months and several sneaky bottles of wine later, they got wed in a modest ceremony in front of Camp Bastion's chaplain. She and Thomas flittered between bases as often as they could, but one of their romantic liaisons led to something unexpected. In the harsh, rocky plains of Afghanistan, Sarah had gotten pregnant with an American Lieutenant. They would be a family—albeit, one separated by gunfire, hostile territory, and nationality.

Thomas had decided that the only way to be together was to quit the Army. Surprisingly, Sarah had been more than happy to oblige. The thought of playing homemaker was appealing to her, and she gave notice to leave the British Army two weeks ago while Thomas was almost out of his contract with the United States. Their future in motion, soon they would begin a life together in sun kissed Florida. The only thing Sarah had left to fear was informing her CO that she'd gotten pregnant in the line of duty. It was frowned upon, to say the least.

"Eyes on," said her Glaswegian corporal, Hamish Barnes. The hulking lad, with the beaten face of a regimental boxing champion, had the wheel of the Land Rover Snatch-2. Sarah sat beside him. In the back were three privates still in nappies, and Sergeant Ernie Miller. The Helmand village of Larurah lay ahead. It was a confirmed 'friendly' village, but that meant little out here in the desert. Allegiances shifted overnight in Afghanistan.

They were on their way to meet with a village elder and his wife, who had potential information on an influential Taliban leader, Al Al-Sharir. Sarah had been sent as the liaison because she had a knack for sorting out the lies from the truth. She was to meet up with the female engagement squad at the far side of the village. The engagement squad would be accompanied by two patrol squads to keep them safe.

Female soldiers couldn't go anywhere in the desert without an escort. Strictly speaking, the British Army didn't like sending women into the field, but Sarah had a way of interacting with the locals, prodding at them and making them drop their guards. Her CO, Major Burke, was enlightened enough to treat Sarah based on her ability, not on her sex, so she would often travel alone with only her squad as protection. She guessed her father's name had much to do with the special treatment.

Little was known about Al-Sharir, but the native Afghan had taken responsibility for a host of recent attacks against British and American personnel. He hadn't claimed association with the Taliban, yet he'd been spotted with several known members in the region. One week ago, Al-Sharir had commanded a small insurgency that had resulted in an American transport truck being flipped by an antique soviet RPG-7. Three servicemen had died, and a fourth had gone back to his family without his left arm. Finding Al-Sharir had become one of the campaign's biggest priorities after finding Bin Laden himself.

Up ahead, several villagers gathered in front of a banged-up Toyota Corolla. The vehicle's white paint had rusted, and the front wheels were missing. The villagers were using it as a place to sit and spectate. With little means of entertainment, it was something for them to do. Having been liberated from the

Taliban, the village was now unoppressed, but many still felt the constraints of fear. The Taliban was a looming presence over the country and many feared reprisals. The people here still weren't free, even after being liberated.

Ahead, there was an overturned watermelon cart in the middle of the road. A lone woman stumbled, trying to pick up the spilled fruit and tripping over her burkha. No men offered to help her. Because she was a woman.

"Halt here," said Sarah. "We're going to help."

Hamish glanced at her and frowned.

"Just do it," she snapped at him. She hadn't fought her way to Captain to watch ignorant men ignore a woman in need.

"Is there a problem, captain?" Sergeant Miller stepped out the rear of the Snatch and joined up with her. He looked concerned.

"Help me get this fruit cart back on its wheels."

"Do we have the time?"

"We'll make time," Sarah snapped. "Now come on."

Miller nodded and moved up beside the cart, taking hold of one side, waiting for Sarah to grab the other. Men and women watched from a dozen nooks and crannies, but there were no children playing, which was strange. The local kids were always interested in soldiers arriving.

The woman in the burkha bowed and stepped out of their way, moving over by an old well. As Sarah glanced at the woman, she noticed the missing left hand. Sarah wondered which man had taken it from her: her father, her brother, or some random male who felt he had the right to maim a woman?

"You ready?" asked Miller. "This thing looks like it weighs a shit-ton."

Sarah nodded and grabbed the other side of the watermelon cart.

Miller started a countdown. "After three, ready? One... two..."

Sarah glanced at the woman standing by the well and noticed her eyes narrow and crinkle at the edges, almost as if she were smiling. Or even laughing at them.

"Three!"

Sarah leapt back, but before she had chance to warn her sergeant, Miller lifted the watermelon cart.

Something clicked and then exploded.

Sarah felt herself take flight. Her body was weightless. Her senses merged into a confused blur. She didn't know which way her body was facing when she hit the dirt, but she knew that she didn't want to get up.

The world came rushing back in a maelstrom of colour and sound. First, she saw the watermelon cart ablaze. Second, she saw Miller lying dead less than a dozen yards away, both legs missing, and a pool of blood soaking the ground beneath him.

Gunfire—*clatter clatter*—filled the air.

Sarah felt weightless again. Her body left the ground. At first she thought she'd been captured, heading to some nightmarish fate, but then she heard Hamish's reassuring voice in her tinging ears.

"You're gun' be right, Captain. Everything's gun' be right."

Sarah Groaned. "Miller?"

"He's gone. We need to bolt."

Hamish dragged Sarah over to the Snatch where the three privates were providing nervous covering-fire. This reminded Sarah that she was in charge. The men needed her to take them to safety. It was her fault they were in this situation.

"Everyone, back inside the Snatch," she commanded, back in control of herself. "We're getting out of here, now."

The three privates fired off a short burst of gunfire from

their SA80s, then threw themselves into the rear of the armoured Land Rover. Hamish took the wheel and Sarah pulled herself in beside him. Before he started the engine, however, the corporal gave her a worried glance, examining her.

"Everything will be fine," she said. "We'll be sharing a pint down the NAAFI before the day is through."

Hamish nodded, but his craggy face was pale. His thick bottom lip quivered.

Sarah thumped the dashboard. "Sodding move it!!"

Hamish gunned the engine and shot them into reverse. He pulled on the handbrake and spun the vehicle around, but by the time he'd shifted into first, ready to speed away, insurgents had lined the road, blocking their exit. They fired their AK-47s and a swarm of bullets hit the Snatch's reinforced windscreen and grill.

Sarah clenched her fists. "Shit! They will rip us to pieces. Turn us around! We'll head through the village."

Hamish spun the Snatch around again, giant tyres crunching over watermelon and splintered wood. From the top cover, the three privates returned fire.

A cloud of dust coughed up behind the Snatch as they picked up speed.

"Watch the well," Sarah shouted as Hamish drove within feet of the crumbling brick reservoir. The woman who'd tricked them was now firing a hunting rifle at them with careful aim. She used the stump of her left arm as a rest for the barrel.

The woman faded into the distance as Hamish brought the Range Rover up to sixty.

Sarah's hands were shaking. Blood dripped down her shirt and onto her arms. She reached forward and unfolded the Snatch's sun visor and mirror. A wounded stranger stared back at her. The left side of her face was blackened and bloody. Muscle and tendon glistened within a deep crevice of flesh. A shard of wood lay embedded in her cheek, but was too deep to extract.

Sarah fought back revulsion and tried to stay focused. It was a nasty wound, sure to leave at least a small scar, but it wasn't as severe as it could have been. She could have died. Miller had.

The thought of death made Sarah woozy. Her hand shot to her belly as overwhelming horror took over her—fear for her unborn child. Hamish's voice brought her back from the brink of panic.

"Which way?" Hamish asked her, his usual gravel voice now high-pitched and overwrought. "Captain, which way?"

Sarah looked around. The village was a maze of alleyways and crumbling, flat-topped buildings, each one a hiding spot for an RPG or high-powered rifle. Death could come at them a dozen ways. "Go... go... go left. Left, damn it!"

Hamish spun the wheel and whipped the Snatch around to the left, slotting the vehicle into an alleyway between a mosque and a two-story domicile. Villagers leapt into doorways, yelling out insults as they avoided the giant tyres of the Range Rover. Some threw stones, bouncing off the bonnet. Hamish put his foot down.

Gunfire faded behind them.

The three privates pulled themselves back inside the Snatch's rear cabin and sat, panting and gibbering with relief. The battle was over, they were home free.

Sarah put her fingertips to her face and winced at the pain. Now that the danger was over, she freaked out. *Miller is dead and I'm hurt. I need to know that my baby is okay.* She clutched her stomach and sobbed.

Hamish glared at her. "Get your shit together, Captain."

Sarah choked back a sob and nodded. "I... I screwed up. This is all my fault."

Hamish kept his eyes forward, concentrating on the dirt road. "Way I see it, the witch with the watermelons is to blame. I don't know about you, but I'm coming back here with the Second Royals to flatten this place into dust. Focus on that, not on what you could have done."

Sarah nodded. He was right. There was nothing to be done now, but respond to the situation. She needed to get back and report. She needed to check on her baby. Camp Bastion awaited, less than two hours away.

"Step on it," Sarah said, gritting her teeth as shock gave way to lucid pain and rising agony. "The sooner we get out of here, the sooner we can come back and rain hell down on this goddamn village."

"Amen to that," said Hamish, flooring the accelerator. He pulled right, putting the village behind them.

The last thing Sarah saw was the horizon disappearing from the windscreen as the nose of the Snatch rose into the air, riding on a blanket of roaring flames, before crashing back down on its roof.

4

THE CUCKOO'S NEST

Sarah bucked forwards and gasped. For a second, she thought she'd been struck by that IED all over again. When she saw Howard staring back at her from the cockpit, she registered where she was.

"You okay, Sarah?" Howard asked.

"Fine. Just a dream."

"It was good timing, you waking up now. We've arrived."

Sarah went to look out the window, but remembered they were blacked-out. "Where are we?" she asked.

Howard smirked. "Not until you sign the paperwork."

Sarah rolled her eyes, then rubbed at them. Her cheap, yet ever-reliable, Casio watch informed her she'd been asleep for thirty minutes.

The helicopter tilted forward and rotated, losing altitude. Despite his lumbering appearance, Mandy kept impressive control over the aircraft and brought them down smoothly. When they touched earth, Sarah barely felt it.

Howard hopped out of the front passenger seat and slid the rear passenger door open. Sunlight flooded in and Sarah shielded her eyes as she got out.

"Good day for it," Howard said.

"That remains to be seen." Green fields and trees stretched for miles, in every direction. "We're in the middle of nowhere," she noted.

"Not as far from civilisation as you might think, but we have our privacy, that's for sure."

Sarah turned another circle, hoping to catch something she might have missed the first time around, but there was nothing. "Why have you brought me to an empty field?" she asked.

Mandy stepped out from behind the helicopter and stood beside Howard like a marble statue. Howard pulled a small tablet from inside his jacket and held it to his ear. "We're here," he said and ended the call.

There was a sudden vibration followed by a clunk.

Howard moved to a patch of weeds, kicking them flat. After a few moments, he reached and grabbed at something—a wooden hatch, scraps of soil and clumps of mud sliding off of it as it opened.

A gaping hole now lay in front of them.

"Welcome to the Earthworm," Howard said.

Sarah raised an eyebrow. "Earthworm? What the hell is that?"

"It's just what we call it. Its real name is MCU Facility One."

"How many other facilities are there?"

"None."

Sarah cleared her throat. "So why give it a number?"

"Originally, there were going to be more," Howard explained.

"What happened?"

"The banks collapsed. There were two more sites halfway-built, but the economic crises meant that the funding for the projects fell through. MCU Facility One is the only site that got built to completion."

"So, this hole in the ground is... what? A secret base?"

Howard smiled. "Why don't we find out?"

Sarah shrugged. "Sod it, I came this far."

Howard led her over to the opening in the ground while Mandy stayed behind with the helicopter. There was a long staircase before them, heading deep into the ground.

"After you," Howard said.

Sarah was happy to take the lead for a while. She was tired of following like a confused child.

Howard pulled the hatch back into place above them and the sunlight disappeared. LED strip lighting illuminated the staircase, but there was no heating, and it got colder as they descended. Sarah felt claustrophobic, a hundred tons of soil ready to bury her.

"You okay?" Howard asked.

Sarah tried to take a deep breath. "Yeah, I'm fine, just not a fan of confined spaces."

"We'll be at the facility soon."

"Good. Why is this place buried underground, anyway? Even MI5 has an office on the Thames."

Howard sniffed. "MI5 is known to exist, our agency is not. It was set up in response to the 9/11 terrorist attacks as a joint enterprise between the US and UK governments. Its purpose is to provide a joint-run task force that can follow up leads on both continents rapidly and cohesively. The US had three facilities of its own until recently, but this is the only one we have on our side of the Atlantic. We share whatever intel we have with the Pentagon, and they with us. There are no secrets between our two governments under the purview of this task force, and we are a united front against all known threats to our nations."

Sarah clip-clopped down the steps, hoping to reach the end soon. "So, it's kind of like a US/UK bromance."

"I suppose you could call it that. One thing we learned after 9/11 was that much could be gained by working in tandem, rather than pursuing only our own interests. President Bush and Prime Minister Blair agreed to commission the MCU and give it autonomy to act as it saw fit, answering only to the president and prime minister themselves. Nowadays, we answer to President Conrad and Prime Minister Breslow."

Sarah whistled. "Those are some swanky connections. You could probably tell me if Elvis is still alive, huh? What about Benny Hill? Who did he leave his millions to? Is the New World Order a thing? Who is Keyser Soze? What's the deal with Kim Kardashian?"

Howard ignored her. They came to the bottom of the long staircase, and Sarah let out a sigh of relief. Howard stepped up to a keypad and thumbed in a code. The console chirped back at him and then a round door slid aside into a hidden alcove. For once, Sarah had nothing to say. In front of her was a vast open space the size of a football stadium. Her claustrophobia disappeared.

"Told you it opened up," said Howard, patting her back. Sarah stumbled forward, her mouth wide open. She gawped at Howard, but he just smirked at her and said, "Welcome to the Major Crimes Unit."

5

TAKING THE TOUR

"Welcome to the Major Crimes Unit."

Howard followed Sarah in, pressing a button on the wall which closed the hatch behind them. The ceilings were fifty-feet high with massive vents. Banks of computers lined every wall, while a desk, large enough to seat twenty people, took up the centre of the room. At one end of the desk was a large monitor.

Sarah glanced around for people, but there was no one. She noticed that all the computers were off. "Where is everyone?" she asked.

"We have offices in the back," Howard said. "Come on, I'll take you there now."

Sarah followed Howard, taking it all in, but the more she concentrated on her surroundings, the less impressive they became. The equipment was not high-tech, as she'd first believed; the monitors were old CRT units, and the desktops were square and clunky. A thick layer of dust covered everything.

"When was this place built?" Sarah asked as they made their way through the rows of computers.

"It was commissioned after 9/11, so it's over ten years old."

"And when was it last used?"

Howard understood Sarah's confusion. "The facility is bigger than we need, so the team confines itself to a smaller section at the front. Reason we call this place the Earthworm is that it's long and narrow—makes it harder to bomb. We just entered through the tail, but we tend to do our work in the head."

At the far end of the room was another hatchway. Sarah then realised the area was not entirely deserted; a lone security guard in black fatigues stood in the entryway.

Howard nodded to the guard as they drew nearer. The guard nodded back.

Sarah looked the man up and down, then said, "What do you do if you want the toilet? Do they give you a bucket?"

The guard said nothing.

"Do you have a bag strapped to your thigh?"

The guard said nothing. Didn't even look at her.

Sarah shrugged her shoulders. "I'm getting the impression that people don't like talking to me."

Howard inputted another code, and the hatchway opened. The area that followed was far more confined. A narrow corridor branched off in several directions, leading to various doorways. Many of the adjacent rooms had glass partition-walls, allowing one to see inside, but Sarah was concerned to see that most of them were as empty as the tail section had been.

"We're still not at the head yet, I take it?" she asked.

"No," said Howard. "This is the middle. It's mostly offices and research rooms here, and the infirmary is just up ahead. We have a doctor on-site who works there. Dr Bennett, you'll meet her later."

"Can't wait."

The Earthworm was huge, but vastly under-utilised. The middle section must have contained four-dozen empty offices, and while they passed it only briefly, the infirmary was large enough to handle a minor epidemic. Must have cost a fortune.

So why not use it?

They came to another hatchway, but there was no guard at this one. Instead, there was a bulky CCTV camera hanging over it. Howard inputted another code, and the door slid away. They headed into what Sarah suspected was the Earthworm's head section. This part of the facility was warm and scented with the heady pong of bleach and air freshener. A corkboard affixed one wall with multi-coloured pins spearing notes and memos in a dozen places.

"Some of us pretty much live here," said Howard as they progressed. "There are dorms for those of us who want to use them."

Sarah frowned. "Bit unusual for a bunch of civil servants. Do *you* stay here?"

"Not usually. I keep a place nearby in the city. Sometimes I stay here, though, if circumstances require."

"We're near a city, then?" said Sarah. "Interesting. We travelled forty minutes from Birmingham by helicopter, so, assuming we flew around 130mph on average, that would most likely put us in Greater London, someplace rural on the outskirts perhaps. The drive here takes you thirty minutes, so, with the traffic in and out of the city..." She put her finger against her lips and thought for a few seconds. "My best guess would be that we're in Uxbridge, or maybe as far out as High Wycombe."

Howard's lip twitched, which let Sarah know she was right—or at least close enough. For once, she was the one smirking at Howard.

Howard changed the subject and ushered her forward. "I suspect everybody is in the briefing room waiting for us."

Unlike the rest of the facility, the following room was high-tech and in obvious use. Paper-thin flat screens lined the walls and blinking apparatuses sat on desks.

Three people sat around a glass table in the centre of the room, but stood when they saw Sarah. The largest of them was a middle-aged Asian man with a shiny, bald head. From the steel bracelet around his right wrist, Sarah assumed he was Sikh. Beside him was a diminutive brunette, with impeccable make-up and a clean, white lab coat. The third person was a mousy-haired bag of bones. He had the gleaming, bright blue eyes of a child, and seemed little older.

They all flinched—a nearly imperceptible shudder in their eyes—when they saw Sarah's scars, but she was so used to the reaction that she didn't even let it worry her anymore.

The Sikh offered his hand. "Ms Stone, thank you for coming."

Sarah shook the man's hand but said nothing.

"I can't say she came entirely willingly," Howard said, "but we got there in the end, didn't we, Sarah?"

Sarah watched the Sikh man, clearly the one in charge. "Why am I here?" she asked him. "I'd like answers."

"My name is Director Palu and I am in charge here at MCU. I assume Howard has shared at least a little about why you've been brought here."

Sarah shrugged. "He told me we were somewhere outside London, near High Wycombe."

Howard spluttered. "I… I never—she guessed."

Director Palu waved his hand dismissively and smiled at Sarah. "Your guess was correct. We're beneath some fallow farmland owned by the Government. It's considered a patch of wasteland to the public, so we're relatively undisturbed."

Sarah was astounded such a place as this existed, but she wasn't about to reveal her surprise. These situations were a power-play. The more she could keep them off their game, the better advantage she'd have.

"Please, take a seat, Ms Stone. Officer Hopkins and I will conduct a quick debrief and be right back with you. In the meantime, please fill out this *Official Secrets Document*. I'm sure you're familiar with one. I'll leave you with Agents Jacobs and Bennett."

Howard and Palu left the room.

Without being asked, Sarah took a seat at the table opposite the skinny kid and scrawled a signature for one *Basil Fawlty* on the OFS document before swatting it aside.

"So, are you here for some work experience?" she asked the kid.

His bony cheeks went red. "N-no, Captain. I work here. Well, sort of. I leave today."

"Leave? Bit young for a career change, aren't you?"

"I'm twenty-four." He glanced at the table. Sarah wondered if he couldn't face her scars. "I'm not cut out for this place," he muttered. "I tried, but..."

"But what?"

"But he screwed up," said the brunette in the lab coat. She had an American accent that reminded Sarah of her late husband's Floridian drawl. "He screwed up a lot."

The kid blushed a deeper shade of red.

"What's your name?" Sarah asked. The kid interested her.

"His name is Bradley Jacobs," answered the American woman.

"And what's your name, sweetheart?" Sarah asked.

"My name is Dr Jessica Bennett, not *sweetheart*."

"Oh, so *you're* Bennett. Look, doctor, I understand that being a git is all the rage in medicine, thanks to Hugh Laurie, but I'm trying to have a conversation with Bradley here, and all I can hear is your yap."

Dr Bennett shot up from her chair and slapped her palms on the glass table. She glared at Sarah, but couldn't keep her gaze for more than a few seconds.

Sarah scowled, to make her scars that bit uglier.

The doctor stormed out of the room, leaving Sarah to fix her gaze on Bradley. The kid struggled to keep eye contact with her. "Do my scars frighten you?" she asked.

"What? No! Why would they?"

"Because it looks like someone lit my face on fire and then wiped their arse with it."

"No, it doesn't. You just look… different. Anyway, your scars don't bother me. They obviously bother you though."

Sarah sniffed, surprised by the comeback. The kid had deflected her button-pushing and prodded back at hers. "So, why are you leaving?" she asked, trying a different tack. "Did you screw up that badly?"

Bradley nodded. "I froze in the field. I was with Agent Hopkins, trying to find intel on a target. We were investigating an old warehouse when a group of men drew on us. I froze and was too late shouting a warning. If it wasn't for the strike team with us, Howard would've got shot."

Sarah shrugged. "It happens, kid. Especially the first time."

"It was my second time. I've frozen twice when it matters. I'm going to get someone killed if I don't leave. Just waiting for the clearances. Today should be my last day."

Sarah felt sorry for Bradley. The kid had a moral centre clear for all to see but lacked confidence in himself. Maybe *his* father was an overbearing bastard as well. "How did you ever end up in this place?" she asked him.

"My father."

Sarah rolled her eyes. "Thought so."

"He was a physicist, worked on some of Britain's first nuclear power plants. He wanted me to do Physics, too, so I did—even got into Cambridge. I specialised in nuclear physics and wrote a paper on the application of nuclear components for the purposes of terrorism. Long story short, the paper raised questions with the Government's counter-terrorism officers, and I was headhunted to join MCU as a theoretical consultant. At first, I thought I would be like James Bond, but it soon became clear that the last thing I am is a hero."

"There's no such thing as heroes," Sarah told him. "Heroes exist in storybooks to convince us that humanity isn't made up of selfish pricks."

Bradley shook his head. "I don't believe that. Deep down, I don't believe you do either, Captain."

Sarah stared at the kid and couldn't help but laugh at his defiant positivity. "All I have deep down is an ulcer. You should stop trying to find the best in people. An attitude like that won't do you any favours."

Bradley shrugged. "You're probably right. At least I'm getting out of here soon. You'll make a good replacement."

Sarah blanched. "What?"

Bradley shrugged. "I assume Howard brought you here to replace me. Today is my last day, and they've got you here. I don't imagine it's a coincidence."

"I came here to help out with a single matter and don't plan on giving you people more than an afternoon of my time. Forgive me if working for the Government isn't exactly an appealing prospect."

"Maybe I'm wrong," said Bradley. "To tell you the truth, nobody's told me anything since I decided to leave."

Sarah's expression softened, at least as much as her scars allowed. She knew how it felt to be abandoned by superiors.

Director Palu and Howard re-entered the room and took a

seat at the table. When Palu realised someone was missing, he frowned. “Did Dr Bennett introduce herself before leaving?”

“Yes,” Sarah said, “she showed me pictures of all her cats.”

Palu chuckled. “Yes, Jessica certainly does love her cats. Her little children, she calls them.”

Sarah grinned. “So, are you going to tell me why you dragged me here like a bunch of cold war spies, or am I going to have to beat it out of someone?”

“Don’t think that worked out too well for you last time,” said Howard, mocking her. “How many times did I knock you down?”

Sarah chuckled. “I like to go a few rounds before knocking the other guy out. You’ll learn that about me, *Howie.*”

Palu let his meaty hands drop to the table, capturing their attention. “Perhaps we should get to the main thrust of things. You’re no doubt curious as to why we brought you here, Ms Stone.”

“Your powers of deduction astound me. I can see why they put you in charge.”

Palu sniffed and a brief glimmer of frustration shimmered across his face. Sarah smiled, pleased that she was getting on his nerves. She couldn’t help but prod at authority.

“You’re aware of the explosion in Knutsford this past Sunday,” Palu said.

Sarah nodded.

“The man responsible is an ex postal worker named Jeffrey Blanchfield. It is believed he had some sort of grudge. He was recently widowed, losing his wife to a massive heart attack. Police reports suggest Jeffrey and his wife were having ongoing issues with their neighbours and local youths. There were reports of vandalism, threats, and regular noise complaints. After Jeffrey’s wife died, he blamed the local youths for her death and confronted them. They responded by cracking his jaw and leaving him with a broken hip. Six months later, Jeffrey blows up a village fete two miles from his home."

"Good for him," Sarah said, but immediately regretted it. It was a stupid thing to say. Even Bradley moaned at the insensitivity.

Palu stared at her. "Forty people dead, Ms Stone. Another eighty injured. It was one of the worst terrorist attacks in our country's history."

Sarah nearly apologised, but decided there was little to be gained from it. "An old man with a vendetta does not a terrorist make," she said. "He wanted to cause pain and suffering, not invoke terror. He had no agenda other than revenge."

"That's where you're wrong, Sarah," Howard said.

Palu nodded. "I think you better watch something we received this morning." He produced a tiny remote control from the breast pocket of his shirt and pointed it at one of the television screens. The TV blinked to life, and a grainy video played. A man with good, yet accented English spoke. He was flanked by two others: a stocky man with hairy arms, and a smaller figure hiding in the shadows to the left.

"People of the United Kingdom, today you have been struck by a warrior. A martyr in the battle for humanity itself. Through Jeffrey Blanchfield's sacrifice, all of you have been given a chance to cleanse your souls of impurity. Reflect upon your nation's depravity and degradation before it is too late. Today, many of you have been taken, and soon more, but if you seek the holy path, all may not yet be lost. My name is Al Al-Sharir, and Allah has given me a divine mission to save you from your own moral annihilation."

Sarah stared hard at the screen. The video feed was grubby, possibly from a VHS cassette tape or film from a low-spec mobile phone. The man who was delivering the message was wearing *shalwar kameez*—loose pajama-like trousers beneath a long tunic. He was also wearing a red and white *shemagh*—a checked headscarf. A symbol of a scimitar emblazoned his right wrist, inked in henna so as not to permanently alter the temple of his flesh. The symbol of the sword was something all members of *Shab Bekheir* wore.

Sarah turned to Palu and shrugged her shoulders. "They're just trying to capitalise on a tragedy. It's terrorism 101."

Palu shook his head. "Just keep watching."

"In twenty-four hours," the man on the video said, "your nation will be hit again. Jeffrey Blanchfield was a martyr, avenging his dead wife who was killed because of your decadent ways. The next attacks will be greater, and we will not stop until Prime Minister Breslow denounces the people of the United Kingdom as heathens and sinners. Only then may you all be saved. *Shab Bekheir* will show you the way."

Howard tapped his fingertips against the glass desk. "The videocassette was sent to Downing Street from the Knutsford postoffice. The postage date was two days before the attack."

"I tried to track down the sender," explained Bradley, "but the postoffice doesn't have CCTV, and the fee was paid in cash."

Sarah leaned back in her chair and let out a long, lingering sigh. There was lots to consider, and many things that made little sense.

"What are your thoughts?" Howard asked her. "The reason I brought you here is that you've dealt with Al-Sharir before, first hand."

"Yes," Palu said. "What do you make of the videotape, Ms Stone?"

Sarah chewed at the side of her cheek. "My first thought," she said, "is that it's a fake."

6

LEARNING THE ROPES

"What do you mean it's fake?" cried Howard, angered by her assertion. "I verified it myself."

"Do you people do this for a living?" she asked them. "No wonder terrorists think they can win."

Howard glared at her, but Palu took over the conversation before an argument erupted. "Why do you think it's a fake, Ms Stone?"

"I don't think it, I know it."

"How?" asked Bradley. "It looks real to me. We've identified the accent as Pashto, which is consistent with members of *Shab Bekhier*. Their origin is the southern regions of Afghanistan, where you served, Captain."

Sarah, for a brief second, doubted herself. It had been a long time since she'd been in the game, and a long time since she'd been in Afghanistan. Did she have cause to be so confident?

Hell yes, she did.

"The first thing telling me that wasn't Al Al-Sharir, is the red and white headscarf that is more common to Jordanians.

Al-Sharir and his men operate in Afghanistan. They would wear *Pakol* or *Lungee.*"

"That's a bit of a stretch," said Howard in a voice patronising enough she wanted to punch him.

"Fair enough. Then how about the fact that the man standing to the right of the frame is white? His hands and wrists are visible and you can see tufts of fair hair on his forearm. Al-Sharir might take advantage of a grieving old man to blow up a village, but I doubt he would work closely with a westerner. He's too much of an extremist. To him, we're two different species, two different animals fighting for supremacy. He wouldn't trust someone he considered part of another tribe."

"That's another big jump," said Palu. "The white man could be a Muslim of mixed birth."

Sarah nodded. "You might be right, but the main reason I know that the man delivering the message is not Al Al-Sharir is because the scimitar on his wrist is pointing the wrong way. The tip should point at him, not away."

Howard huffed. "It's a henna tattoo. I'm sure Al-Sharir pays little attention to a bit of ink on his arm."

Sarah groaned. "That only proves how incompetent these impostors are and how little you people know about the man you're blaming this on. That tattoo means everything to members of *Shab Bekheir*. Al-Sharir would only ever have the scimitar pointing at himself because it signifies his willingness to die for Allah. It signifies him being a willing martyr. If it pointed the other way, at his enemies, it would signify that *they* were the ones dying for a righteous cause." Sarah folded her arms in front of her chest. "You've been played. This whole thing is some kind of dupe. The small details are the ones that matter most."

Palu remained still. He seemed more willing to believe her

now, but there was still a degree of obstinacy in his tone. "How can you be so sure?"

"How can I be so sure? Maybe because I've met Al-Sharir and I know his way of doing things. He pays too much attention to detail to be the guy in that video. I don't know who's behind the attack on Sunday, if it was more than just an angry widow, but I'm telling you it was not Al-Sharir."

Palu rubbed at his forehead and then stood up. "Okay, let me check a few things out. Howard, Bradley, a moment, please?"

All three men left the room.

They left Sarah alone for more than an hour. For all she knew, they were planning on leaving her there all day. Patience wasn't a virtue of hers, so she decided to interrupt them. She had a life to get back to—a shitty life, but one she preferred to waiting around for a bunch of government pricks to take her seriously. She'd already helped out more than she'd intended.

When she'd thought there had been a chance to help take down Al Al-Sharir, she had been willing, maybe even eager to assist, but it looked like it had been a wild goose chase.

Sarah headed in the same direction the men left and found the door unlocked. She stepped into the following corridor and realized there was another half-dozen rooms leading off to both sides.

The sound of voices led her to the second door on the left. Sarah was planning to shove her way inside when she realized she could make out the conversation from the corridor.

"She's a liability," Palu said. "It was a mistake bringing her here, Howard. I should never have authorised it."

"I know," said Howard. "I assumed she'd jump at the chance to get away from her pathetic life, but she's done nothing but fight me. She's not the woman she was in the Army. She's a mess."

"Guys, you're missing the point," Bradley said. "Captain Stone was right; the man in that video isn't Al Al-Sharir. You brought her here to offer her expertise on Shab Bekhier, and that's exactly what she's done. I think she'll make a great replacement for me. You need someone that's faced these monsters on their own turf, someone with real experience."

Palu grunted. "What are you talking about, Bradley? She's not going to replace you. We needed her expertise, and we've gotten it. The sooner we send her on her way, the better."

"Oh, so who will replace me, then?"

"No one," said Palu. "The cost to train another Officer is too high. To tell you the truth, it's unfortunate things didn't work out with you, Bradley, as we will be left even more short-handed now."

"Sorry."

"Nothing that can be done now. Your clearances have come through, and you're free to leave as soon as we finish with Ms Stone," said Palu.

"Captain Stone," Bradley corrected. "I think if you showed her some respect she'd be more helpful. She's given up a lot for her country and has nothing to show for it. Asking for her help isn't enough, we need to earn it from her. She was a Captain in the British Army, and she was wounded fighting for our country, facing the very enemy we're trying to stop now. Don't you think her help will come in handy?"

Howard disagreed. "We don't need her help. It was a mistake me bringing her here. She's been nothing but a pain. I thought she'd be... different."

"You mean you thought she'd be grateful," said Bradley. "That's the problem. You're acting like you're the one doing her a favour, when really it's the other way around."

"Let's get back to the conference room," Palu said. "We've already been too long."

Sarah flinched away from the doorway. She thought quickly and rushed back to the conference room rather than betray that she'd been listening. The more she knew, and the less they did, the better.

The office door opened. Sarah slipped back into the conference room just as Palu and the others stepped into the hallway. By the time they got to the conference room, Sarah was sitting with her boots up on the desk. "You chimps finished your tea party?"

Palu cleared his throat and remained standing. "It appears you were right... *Captain.* We have accessed existing surveillance footage of Al-Sharir and reviewed previously verified footage of Shab Bekhier. You're right, the details don't match. Based on that, we're assuming that Sunday's attack was the work of someone else. Perhaps the videotape itself is the act of terror, hoping to put us all on high alert."

"Probably," said Sarah. "If a suicide bomb in Cheshire wasn't enough."

Palu sighed. "With all of our technology and surveillance, the one thing we can't do is police every person on the planet. The fact the bomber was an elderly white man meant we were unprepared. He didn't exactly fit our profile of an extremist."

"One thing I know about crazy," said Sarah, "is that it doesn't wear a uniform or keep set hours. You can't profile hate. It can infect anyone."

"Do you think there will be further attacks, Captain?" asked Bradley. "What's your gut feeling?"

Sarah pulled her boots off the desk and looked at them. "I'm not sure. If the men in the video are organised enough to be behind Sunday's attack, then perhaps there's still a threat, but why would they hide behind a charade, pretending to be

Shab Bekhier? If the real Al-Sharir finds out somebody's using his name, they're signing their own death warrants within the terrorist community. Best case scenario, it's somebody trying to exacerbate an already distressing situation. Maybe a small group of extremists talked Jeffrey Blanchfield into blowing himself up. Perhaps that's all there is to it."

"I hope you're right," Palu said. "I thank you for your help, Captain. It was enlightening."

"Yes," said Bradley. "You know your stuff."

"Thank you." Sarah couldn't be a bitch to Bradley. He was a scolded puppy. Plus, he'd stood up for her in the other room, and she owed him for that.

"I'll take you back up top," Howard told her. "Mandy will take you where you want to go."

"I've always wanted to go to Disney World," said Sarah. "I hear they have a giant golf ball you can ride around in."

"Domestic flights only, I'm afraid," Howard said.

"Come on, then. The sooner I get out of this place, the sooner I can get the government stink off me."

There was a sudden electronic chirping. Everyone looked to Palu who plucked a small tablet from his trouser pocket. With his free hand, he motioned for Howard and Sarah to get going. Sarah was more than happy to oblige; her claustrophobia was returning. She was just about to leave when she noticed Palu's face became horror-stricken.

Howard tried to pull Sarah away, but she shrugged him off and remained standing by the glass conference table.

Palu muttered into the phone. "When, sir? I understand, sir. We had no intel concerning that. I... yes, I agree, sir. I'll await your instructions." He hung up.

"What is it?" Howard asked. "Who was on the call?"

Palu shook his head and looked like he was going to throw

up. “There’s been another attack,” he said. “Another suicide bombing.”

Howard kicked a nearby chair. “Damn it! Where?”

Palu closed his eyes and looked sick. “Three more villages —Studley, Dartmouth, Arborfield—all hit within ten minutes of each other. Downing Street is still getting all the information they can; they’ll forward it to us.”

Sarah bent forward, leaning on the table. Three villages all at once? The country was under attack.

Bradley looked close to tears. “It makes little sense, hitting tiny villages in lieu of bigger targets. What’s the significance?”

Sarah knew. “It means nobody is safe. It means you don’t have to live in London or Manchester or Birmingham anymore to be the target of a terrorist attack. You can live in the smallest village and still get blown up. It’s smart, if you think about it. Terrorists want to cause terror. What better way than to make the entire country afraid of being attacked? No place is safe anymore, and the public will know it. The whole of the United Kingdom is about to become terrified.”

“Shit,” Bradley said.

“Yeah,” Sarah agreed. “Shit is the right word, because it just hit the fan.”

7

SITTING THE TEST

Palu turned on the television, and a breaking news report came on. A BBC journalist stood before a scene of devastation.

The quaint fishing village of Dartmouth was aflame. Its picturesque harbour had become ground zero of a devastating attack. Bodies cluttered the marina floating face down in the water. Further out, a blackened ferry sank into the River Dart's estuary, yachts and pleasure cruisers sinking with it. Dogs howled from the wooden jetties while shell shocked survivors wept in the street. An ash-covered child wandered around with no parent or guardian to watch her. The little girl cried out for her mummy.

The reporter wiped a tear from his eye and cleared his throat before speaking. "T-Today, as I report to you, I am lost for words. After the events of this past Sunday, Britain was a nation already in mourning. Yet, today, the tragedy worsens as yet another mass killing has occurred. Worse still, the village of Dartmouth behind me was not the only target. The villages of Studley and Arborfield have also been hit by what appears to be a co-ordinated terrorist attack. Whether today's atrocities are linked to Sunday's incident in the village of Knutsford is, as yet, unclear, but the death toll and devastation Britain has witnessed in the last forty-eight hours is the worst in its entire history. The Prime Minister is due to give a speech within the hour, but right now, the question on everybody's mind is: who is behind this? I'm Jack Millis, reporting to you from the village of Dartmouth, Devon."

Sarah felt winded. If anything, Britain had started to put the fear of terrorism behind it. Bungled attempts at carrying bombs aboard planes in shoes and other useless attempts had reduced the modern-day terrorist to a cartoonish villain foiled at every turn. They had become fodder for South Park and Private Eye newspaper—a joke, not a threat.

Someone had screwed up. Sarah clenched her fists as she thought about the three men in the room. This was their job. They were supposed to stop things like this from happening. "Did you people know anything about this? Was there anything you could have done? Did you let this happen?"

Palu answered the question in a firm, authoritative voice. "No, we did not. If there was anything we could have done, we would have."

Sarah shook her head and tried to understand. "You tell me that your job is to catch terrorists, so how the hell did this happen?"

Bradley still had tears in his eyes. "Captain, I promise you we do all we can."

"Shut up!" Sarah shouted. "People are dead because none of you caught this. Why did you people even bring me here? You're too late. The damage is done."

Palu strode towards Sarah. For a moment, it looked as though he might strike her, but instead he looked her square in the eye. "If you think we're all a bunch of idiots, Captain, then help us. Help us find who's responsible."

"No," Sarah said. She couldn't help these people. They were under manned and ignorant. And she was... broken, and of no use to anyone. They called her Captain, but the truth was she was nothing anymore. The thought of diving back into that dangerous world, filled with murderous men and their callous actions, was enough to make her feel faint. Her father has warned her not to get involved in such serious business, and when she'd defied him, she'd paid for it. She wasn't stupid enough to do it a second time. She turned towards the door.

"Sarah!" Palu shouted. "Before you leave, let me show you something."

Sarah turned around. "What? You people don't even want me here. I heard you talking about me in the other room."

Palu stared her right in the eyes. There was sadness there, but something much darker bubbling beneath. "I just got the stats on the latest attacks," he said. "You should see them before you decide." He pointed the remote at the television. "I may have wanted you gone," Palu said, "but right now, we need all the help we can get. You have knowledge of Shab Bakhier that we can use. Can you really walk away, knowing you could help us?"

Sarah stared at the figures on the screen.

UK TERRORIST ATTACKS, MAY 2014

Kuntsford: 40 fatalities (6 children), 86 injured
Arborfield: 36 fatalities (2 children), 47 injured
Dartmouth: 94 fatalities (19 children), 119 injured
Studley: 12 fatalities (2 children), 4 injured

— Total deceased: 182 (29 children)

"Okay," she said. "I'm in."

8

READY FOR ANYTHING

Everybody took a seat at the conference table. Dr Bennett had been recalled from the infirmary and didn't look happy. According to Palu, the American woman was an expert in bio-terrorism, profiling, and medicine.

Bradley had been asked to collect his things and leave. As his duty had expired, they could no longer share classified information with him. That didn't sit well with Sarah. She knew that resigning from active service was a long-winded affair, and it had doubtlessly been in the works for weeks before she'd arrived, but without the option of replacing Bradley, it seemed wasteful to let him go. Palu had said he needed all the help he could get.

Palu's tablet hadn't stopped beeping since they'd looked at the statistics on screen. Every message the man received made him tenser until he had resembled a coiled spring. Sarah felt sorry for him. He may have been in charge of MCU, but he was clearly a mutt with many masters.

"Prime Minister Breslow has just given a speech from Downing Street," Palu informed them. "She's halted the exit-strategy for Afghanistan and is even reinforcing the number of troops in the region. She's keen to display Britain's strength. A request for aid has been made to President Conrad."

Howard huffed. "The yanks won't go for it. The American people are tired of war. Conrad will leave us hanging, I guarantee it. Loyalty is a one-way street with the Americans. They think helping out in World War II earned them enough brownie points to last a century."

"That's a little unfair," Bradley said, entering from the back of the room with his things. "The Americans have aided us countless times."

"Really?" said Howard. "So where are they now? MCU is supposed to be a joint enterprise, but it's been over a year since they made any contribution to our cause."

"They gave you me," Dr Bennett said, aggrieved. "That's hardly *nothing*."

He rolled his eyes. "You were a token gesture. The US closed their own MCU facilities, and their funding has dropped through the floor."

Bennett folded her arms. When she spoke this time, her tone was angry and her accent stronger. "Do not refer to me as a *token*. I'm the most qualified person in this whole damned facility. Believe me, I'd sooner be back home if y'all have no further need of my services."

"You are highly valued," said Palu. "Now more than ever."

Dr Bennett nodded at the director, apparently satisfied.

"What's the deal here?" Sarah butted in. "I mean, why is this place abandoned? Why is there a skeleton crew inside a place that must have cost millions? There was a single guy guarding the entrance, for Christ's sake."

"They're closing us down, Captain," said Palu. "Not this minute, not this month, but the writing is on the wall. After 9/11, the CIA, FBI, Police, Interpol, MI5 & 6, Scotland Yard, and the Army... they were all given huge additional funding and free-reign. It was messy, to say the least. The MCU was intended to bring things together, to stop the in-fighting and bring cohesion to the US and UK counter-intelligence operations."

Sarah's eyes narrowed. "So, what happened?"

"The economy happened. Other agencies resented our funding and held back their intel, refusing to co-operate. The MCU became benign and costly. In the last six years, we have been scaled back by nine-tenths and been stripped of most of our authority. Most of our intel we get from our contacts within the other agencies. We live off their scraps, where the initial plan was for MCU to be at the centre of everything. Regardless, we still do everything we can to help protect this country."

"So why the hell are you letting Bradley go?" Sarah asked, nodding to the kid.

"I decided to leave, Captain," said Bradley, lingering by the exit.

Sarah didn't care. "Having a member of an already under manned team quitting is bullshit."

"It's already done," said Palu.

"Then undo it. You want my help, then Bradley stays. The more able bodies you have, the better. Wouldn't you agree?"

"Fine," muttered Palu. "Bradley, your resignation is hereby denied. You are to return to work immediately, until such time that the current crisis is resolved. Sarah, you too are operating on a limited mandate. We will discuss your role here in greater depth once we deal with the current situation."

"Whoop-de-do."

Bradley took a seat back at the table, looking nervous but committed.

Howard rolled his head on his shoulders and let out a sigh. "So," he said, "what do we have?"

"Not much," Palu said. "The Army has bomb specialists going through each location as we speak. It looks like more suicide vests from early witness reports. The Upper Ferry was the target in Dartmouth; a local pub in Studley; and in Arborfield a supermarket was hit. I'm getting statements for all three attacks and CCTV footage from the pub in Studley."

Sarah frowned. "You did all that from your phone?"

Palu nodded. "It's a mobile sat link with a proprietary operating system. We've been scaled back, but I can still access the Government's internal systems. Anything the police or other UK agencies have, I can get. We even have limited access to the FBI and CIA. Our biggest asset, however, is our liaison: Downing Street."

Sarah was impressed. Most of what she'd seen of the MCU had been pitiful, but now it was gaining her respect. "Do we have any files on Jeffrey Blanchfield?" she asked. "We need to know if he had any connections to known terrorist groups."

"Maybe he was part of Al-Qaeda's over-60 cell," Dr Bennett quipped.

"Maybe," said Sarah, acting as if she hadn't noticed the American woman's sarcasm and giving back some of her own by mocking her Georgian accent. "There's a fine chance this here attack was connected to today's commotion. If it is, then old Jeffrey has a done rubbed shoulders with some mighty bad people."

Dr Bennett scowled.

"I agree," said Bradley, oblivious to the cold war going on between the two women. "We need to know if there's a link between Sunday's attack and today's. I'll get on it right now." He pulled a wafer-thin laptop out of his satchel and began typing away.

"Get me the CCTV footage for the pub in Studley as well," said Palu. "Apparently there's clear footage of the suicide bomber."

Something on Howard beeped. "There's been another video," he said looking at his phone. "Released on the Internet, this time. It already has a million hits on ClipShare."

"They must be angry that we kept their first video secret," Dr Bennett said. "They want to make sure they get credit this time."

Sarah sighed. "Now they can claim the Government kept the cause of Sunday's attack secret. It's a good way to sow even more discord."

"Put the video on the big screen, Howard," Palu instructed. "It's the only thing we have to work with for the moment."

This time, the three men in the video were not wearing headscarves. They wore red bandanas over their mouths instead. Each was also wearing matching army fatigues. Sarah couldn't be sure, but the uniforms looked like British Army, issued in the eighties perhaps. Her father had worn something similar during the Falkland's conflict.

In the background of the video was a single desk holding a dusty old lamp. There was nothing else to see except brick wall and an unidentified light source overhead. It swung and tilted as if a ceiling bulb were swinging to-and-fro.

The man at the front of the shot began his speech, his voice gravelly and thick beneath his bandana. His eyes were a deep brown and soulless. "People of the UK, today begins your reckoning. Your villages burn like those set aflame by your own government. The time for you to taste your own medicine has come. Your trinkets and idols will be taken from you, death and misery left in their place. You will suffer, as innocent people around the world have suffered under your country's amoral boot-heel for centuries. We are watching your soldiers, your agents, and your murderers-for-hire all around the world. Every time they take a life, we will take more, that is our pledge. The four villages set ablaze are payback for a decade of murder in Afghanistan. You kill, we kill. Remove your soldiers, and the killing will stop. Have your Prime Minister renounce Britain's imperialistic past and its greed-soaked present, and we will disband. Until that time, we are humanity's army, fighting for the future. *Shab Bekheir* will show you the way. Sometimes death is the only way to ensure life."

There was silence in the room for several minutes while they let things sink in.

Palu's phone's beeping broke the silence. "The Prime Minister has just responded to the most recent tape," he told them. "She promises the terrorist's actions will not go unanswered and that Great Britain does not bend to threats." He shook his head. "The media are in uproar, warning against a war on UK soil. They've caught wind of the first tape being suppressed and are citing the Government's incompetence as the reason three more attacks were able to happen."

"There will be panic," Bradley said in a strained voice.

"I need to contact Homeland," Dr Bennett said, standing up to leave the room. "See if President Conrad will make a statement of support."

Bradley zapped something over to the television screen. It was the black and white CCTV feed from the pub in Studley. It showed a middle-aged woman wearing a long black cardigan. She'd just entered the bar of a typical bistro pub and was casually looking around. It was a place more eatery than boozer—the money was in the grub these days. It made a strange target for a terrorist attack.

"What are we looking at, Bradley?" Howard asked.

"This is CCTV video footage taken from the Barley Mow

pub in Studley," he explained. "The local police have cleaned up the image as best they can and cut the footage down to the two minutes before the explosion. We have everything except sound."

The woman in the video wandered into the middle of the pub's dining area. A few seconds later, she ripped open her cardigan and shouted something. The video's resolution was too low to make out what was around her waist, but it was obvious from the frightened screams of the victims. The bomb vest exploded, and the CCTV feed ended.

Everybody in the conference room groaned, even Sarah.

"An initial background has been compiled," said Howard. "The bomber's name was Caroline Pugh. She was white, middle-aged, and worked a full-time job as a legal secretary. I'm working on getting a deeper background, but so far, she doesn't appear to be a typical terrorist either."

"What is a *typical* terrorist?" Sarah asked.

Howard sighed. "You know what I mean. I'm not being racist, just realistic. At the very least, you would expect a terrorist to be from another country, or part of a group with an agenda. Jeffrey Blanchfield and Caroline Pugh were average UK citizens. It doesn't make any sense. How do they connect to Shab Bekhier and the man in the videotape?"

"I don't know," Sarah admitted. "But I know who the man in the videotape is."

Everyone stared at her. Bradley stopped typing.

Sarah thought of the man she'd just watched onscreen. She hadn't been positive of his identity until he'd spoken his final words: *Sometimes only death can ensure life.* "The man in the tape is Wazir Hesbani," she said. "I'd know his face anywhere, because he's the man who took mine."

. . .

AFGHANISTAN, 2008

Sarah blinked. She took a deep breath, but instead of oxygen she got smoke and fumes. A rising pressure in her head threatened to split her skull, and she realised she was upside down, hanging by her seatbelt.

Everything came rushing back. The woman, the watermelons, Miller ripped apart by an explosion, and then white light followed by utter darkness.

Had they hit an IED?

Sarah craned her neck and glanced around inside the Land Rover. She saw shapes in the darkness. "Hamish. Hamish? Anyone? Sound off."

There was nothing, just silence and smoke. Sarah was lucky to be alive. She needed to know which of her men were still breathing and get them the hell out of there.

She pulled out the small flick-blade she kept on her belt and wished it was a machete, but it would have to do. With it she sawed at the strap around her waist, gritting her teeth as she did so. There was a white hot burning in her left thigh but, in the darkness, she couldn't see the cause.

Voices.

For a moment, Sarah thought that one of her squad had awoken, but then she realised the voices were coming from further away. After what had happened, the approaching strangers were more likely enemies than friends. *Why do they hate us so much?*

Sarah ground her teeth and swore through pursed lips. She sawed harder at the seatbelt and had to blink as either sweat or blood filled her eyes. Her face throbbed as badly as her leg, and she remembered her reflection in the Snatch's visor. There had been an open wound beneath her left eye, halfway down her cheek.

"Hamish... anybody? If you're breathing, now is the time to look lively."

Silence.

"Damn it!" Sarah had sliced halfway through her belt now, but the voices outside were getting closer. Only minutes before they were right on top of her.

The nylon seatbelt held itself together by one last thread. Then, finally, it snapped. Sarah slipped free. Her head hit the roof panel of the Land Rover and her teeth clacked together, but she shook away the stars and locked her jaw.

The voices were right on top of her now.

Sarah snapped into action. Her training and instincts made her focus on the task at hand—not the pain and fear. There would be time to cry later. She slipped her hand to her waist and slid her sidearm out of its holster—a SIG Sauer L105A1 9mm—and thumbed the safety off.

One last time, she shouted out. "Hamish! Hamish, are you awake?"

Still no answer. She thought she heard a shuffling behind her, but there was no time to investigate. She straightened out her legs and shuffled towards the opening where the Snatch's windscreen used to be. Bits of glass and jagged stones dug into her shins and elbows as she crawled, but she moved fast. Even now she could hear the strangers outside chattering to one another and kicking up sand as they rushed towards her.

Sarah rolled onto her side and clutched her SIG, ready to start popping shots at whoever looked like they deserved it most. She clawed her way through the last of the broken windscreen and made it out onto the dusty road. The heat hit her back immediately.

She spotted the body of one of her men. It might have been Hamish, for he hadn't been in the driver's seat when she came to. He was lying on his back, one arm missing and his face gone. Sarah was glad he was dead, instead of screaming in agony and begging for his mother. One of Hamish's biggest fears was finding himself in a wheelchair or a hospice bed. He would rather have lost his life than his legs.

Sarah dragged herself to her feet just in time to meet the approaching crowd. She raised her SIG and prepared to pull the trigger. Her burning legs wobbled beneath her, and blood ran down her face, but her hands were still as stone.

There were children in the crowd, with wide brown eyes and gawping mouths. Their innocence was still intact—clear by their frightened faces—but that innocence was fading fast, due to be washed away by the blood of Sarah and her squad. It was how children got baptised in the desert. They were going to witness an execution, and in that moment Sarah understood: you couldn't stop violence with violence, and you couldn't teach children with bloodshed.

A man stepped out of the crowd, putting a hand up in front of him as he approached Sarah. "Please, we not here to hurt you. You are British, no?"

Sarah nodded. She realised that her hands were no longer still and that her arm and aim were shaking. "Y-you speak English?"

The man nodded and smiled. "I studied at your Oxford University. Economics, yes?"

"I need to get back to Camp Bastion," Sarah said. "If you're friendly, let me go on my way."

"Your Camp Bastion is sixty miles away. The sun is hot, your face and leg are bleeding. You will not make it there."

Sarah glanced at her leg and saw the top of a twisted nail sticking out of her thigh. It must have come from the IED. She was lucky it hadn't entered her skull.

Seeing the cause of the pain in her leg made it hurt worse, as if she could feel the nail clawing its way into her muscle.

The stranger was right: she'd never make it back to camp by foot, but what were her options?

"Give me a car," she said. "It will be returned later, along with a reward for your assistance."

The young man looked at her like she was a child. "We have nothing. You think we have car? That we believe in British reward? You offer only death and suffering to people of this village. If we help you, Taliban kill us. We help Taliban, British kill us. You are not our friends and you do not offer reward. Only Allah can provide justice for our actions. We all get what is deserved."

"If you don't help me, I'll die. Will Allah provide you justice for murder?"

The man continued smiling, but there was something predatory about the way he was looking at her. "Sometimes death is the only way to ensure life," he said.

Sarah felt her knees wobble. "I'm sorry for what you people are going through, but we *are* here to help you."

"Afghanistan does not need your help."

Sarah noticed blood dripping on the sand next to her foot.

"Your face is bleeding," said the young man. "Let me help you."

Sarah staggered backwards and held her SIG steady, aiming it at the man's face. "No! I need to get back to camp."

"You need rest. Tomorrow you think about returning to your camp." The man took a stride towards her, closing the gap between them to a few feet. The crowd behind him muttered and mumbled. If Sarah fired on the man, they'd be on her in seconds.

"G-get away from me!" she shouted.

"Let me help you." He spoke softly and reached out to her, revealing the image of a dagger on his forearm. "You are bleeding."

"No! Step back, or I will shoot you."

"No, you will not, I think."

Sarah almost called his bluff. She felt the trigger twitch beneath her finger, but pulling it all the way required a strength she didn't have. Her legs folded and she stumbled sideways. She tried to stay on her feet, but her body ached so badly that it was a relief when she hit the dirt and sprawled onto her back.

The young man was on her, yanking the gun out of her hand and ejecting the magazine. He tossed the pistol aside but kept a hold of the ammo. "Your face is very bad," he said. "I need to close wound or infection kill you, no?"

Sarah struggled, but the man straddled her waist and was too heavy to move. "Let me go," she begged. "Who are you?"

The young man held a brass bullet casing in front of her face. "My name is Wazir Hesbani, and I am going to help you, English. Close wound, stop infection, no?" He placed the rear end of the bullet between his teeth and clamped down, twisting at the jacket with his fingers and unscrewing the cap.

Sarah blinked as blood from her face made her vision red. With the man sat on her chest it was hard to breathe.

Wazir spat the brass cap into the dirt, then stared at her with soulless brown eyes. "This might hurt a little." He upended the bullet casing over her face. Sarah spluttered and moaned as the gunpowder covered her wound, stinging and burning, but the pain was nothing compared to what followed.

Wazir pulled a lighter from his pocket and ignited the powder on Sarah's face. The entire left side of her skull crackled, and for a moment, all she could see was flashing whites and yellows. The agony was immense, a thousand push pins shoved into her exposed, scalded flesh.

Finally, a numbness came and everything faded to grey.

Sarah knew she was going to pass out and wished she could fight it, but it was impossible, like trying to fall upwards.

Wazir levelled his face with hers. "There," he said. "It is not pretty, but at least bleeding has stopped." He stood and turned to the crowd. "Take her to Al-Sharir. He will want to talk with her before he hands her over to me."

9

BY STRENGTH AND GUILE

BY STRENGTH AND GUILE

"You're sure the man in the video is Wazir Hesbani?" Palu asked.

Sarah nodded. "Hesbani was Al-Sharir's right-hand man in Afghanistan."

"As part of a terrorist cell?"

"Yes, *Shab Bekheir*. Although, this still doesn't feel like Al-Sharir's work. Bombing innocent civilians, working with westerners... it's not who he is."

Howard frowned. "You keep saying that, but the man is a terrorist."

"He's also a man of rules and principles."

Dr Bennett hissed. "A terrorist has no principles."

Sarah expected nothing less from an American. To them, the world was full of good guys and bad guys, just like their movies, but this was real life, where there were points of view other than the white, Christian hero's. "Most terrorists believe themselves to be warriors," Sarah said. "Principles are *all* they have. We may not understand them or agree with them, but they believe their actions are just. To them, *we* are the terrorists."

Dr Bennett smirked. Sarah ignored it.

"What do you know about Hesbani?" Bradley asked Sarah.

Sarah thought about her dealings with the man and felt sick. "He's a monster. As much as Al-Sharir has principles, Hesbani has none. His role in Shab Bekhier was to do the things that Al-Sharir would not. Hesbani is not a terrorist, he's a psychopath."

"What's his motivation?" Dr Bennett asked. "Typical psychopaths lack the ability to plan and calculate. There seems to have been a lot of thought gone into these attacks."

"Do you think Al-Sharir might still be pulling Hesbani's strings?" Palu asked Sarah.

"I don't know. Al-Sharir attacks soldiers, not civilians. I can see Hesbani acting alone if he had the chance though. He and Al-Sharir would often disagree on methods, so perhaps the cell split up. Al-Sharir wanted to nullify the West's presence in the Middle East. He believes in the rules of war—he wouldn't intentionally attack civilians—but Hesbani lives for revenge. Hesbani wants to hurt the West and have the Middle East rise as a consolidated superpower. He sees himself fighting a great war and emerging as the first true Muslim leader since Saladin."

"But that doesn't tally with what he said on the tape," said Bradley. "He wants the West to withdraw. It sounds like he's trying to *stop* the violence."

"The only way the Middle East can rise," said Howard, "is if the West relinquishes its hold on the region first."

Palu nodded. "So, do we believe that Hesbani's goal is truly what he speaks of? He wants Western forces to withdraw from the Middle East?"

"I think so," said Sarah. "But it wouldn't end there.

Hesbani was raised on hatred for the West. Even if he got what he wanted, he could never live a peaceful life. Without violence, he is nothing. Killing is all he knows. It's his philosophy—sometimes death is the only way to ensure life."

"Then how do we stop him?" asked Bradley. "Do we know where he is?"

"He's here in the country," said Sarah.

"How do you know that?" asked Palu.

"Bring up the video again. I'll show you."

Palu turned on the television and played the video again.

"Pause it there." The video froze. Sarah pointed at the screen. "Look in the background, behind the desk, next to the lamp."

Palu shrugged. "What?"

Bradley tutted, annoyed at himself for not spotting it sooner. "The plug socket. The lamp is plugged into a three-pronged socket."

Sarah nodded. The three black holes were a familiar sight in Britain. They were not something you'd find in the Middle East.

"That narrows it down to several countries," said Palu, "but I would say it's likely a safe bet that Hesbani is in the UK. We need to check flight manifests and Interpol records. See if we can find out when he entered the country and under what name."

Bradley nodded. "Before I do that, I've got some background on Jeffrey Blanchfield."

"Let's see it," said Palu.

Bradley zipped his laptop's display over to the television screen and went through the information with them. "After his wife's death, Jeffrey was involved in several altercations, including assault of a minor, public affray, and reckless endangerment with a motor vehicle. There are numerous reports of him lashing out, particularly at the youths he blamed for his wife's death. He and his wife filed numerous reports of anti-social behaviour around their home prior to her death, but the police could do little."

Despite his monstrous actions, Sarah felt badly for Jeffrey Blanchfield. Sometimes anger could consume a person until there was no room left for things such as compassion or remorse. Sarah knew that all too well.

Bradley clicked onto a new screen. "This is where it gets interesting. Jeffrey was brought before the courts for his consistent offending and ordered to attend grief counselling."

"Why is that interesting?" asked Dr Bennett.

"Because Caroline Pugh was in court-mandated grief counselling, too."

Palu leaned on his elbows and smiled. "Excellent work, Bradley. Do we have anything more on the woman?"

Bradley nodded. "Caroline Pugh, thirty-eight. She lost her daughter to a drunk driver, picked up a drug habit, and was eventually arrested for making a scene at... a local pub. The *Barley Mow*, the same one she blew up."

Bradley continued. "In a prior incident, the pub's barman called the police after Caroline Pugh collapsed on the floor during a cocaine bender. When she refused to get up, he allegedly kicked her so hard that he broke her ribs. He dragged her outside, in front of the whole pub. He got a slap on the wrist for his callous behaviour, but Caroline Pugh was forced into grief counselling to help end her drug addiction—sent to the same court-appointed psychiatrist that Jeffrey Blanchfield was."

Palu hit the desk with his fist. "That's our link! What's the doctor's name? They have to be connected."

Bradley looked over his notes and brought a medical license up on screen. "Wesley Cartwright, MD, Ph.D. He works out of Oxford—I have an address—but conducts court-appointed grief clinics up and down the country. His file is squeaky clean; he lives a quiet life alone. No misdemeanours, no points of interest."

"I don't get it," said Howard. "Why would a psychiatrist be involved with terrorists?"

"Perhaps he doesn't realise he is," said Sarah. "We can't assume anything yet."

"It may just be a coincidence," said Dr Bennett. "The link may be that both suspects were angry and in trouble with the law."

"Perhaps," said Howard. "But somebody got Jeffrey Blanchfield and Caroline Pugh involved in this. Somebody is bringing these people together and brainwashing them into blowing themselves up. Who's behind it all?"

Sarah looked at her chipped fingernails. "I think the United Kingdom is," she said. "Terrorists didn't make Caroline Pugh and Jeffrey Blanchfield broken and angry. We did that; society did that. Terrorists are just taking advantage of what was allowed to happen to these people."

Dr Bennett scoffed. "Nobody did anything to these people. Life is life. We all have the same hardships to deal with. If we all went and blew ourselves up, there'd be none of us left."

"Pain can make people do bad things," said Sarah. "And contrary to popular belief, some people have it worse than others."

"I don't believe that. These people are just insane."

Palu waved his hand. "Stop bickering. It doesn't matter why these people have done what they've done. Our only focus right now is making sure nothing else happens." He turned to Howard. "I need you to track down this Dr Cartwright at his office. So far he's our only solid lead."

"I'm going too," said Sarah.

Palu likely wanted to argue, but he didn't. Maybe it was the look on her face that told him not to. "Fine. You and Bradley can provide support if Howard needs it, but you're to stand down until then."

Sarah snapped off a mock salute. "Aye, Cappin."

Everybody stood. Palu rubbed his hands together and put them against his face. "Dr Bennett and I will work intel while you're gone. Stay on the wire."

Howard nodded and headed out of the room, Bradley and Sarah close behind him. He slipped out his mob-sat and made a call. "Mandy. Get us two road warriors ready to go in five."

Sarah caught up to Howard and looked at him. "Road warriors? Do you have a fleet of tanks here that I missed?"

"Didn't anybody tell you? The Earthworm has arms."

Howard and Bradley led Sarah into the Earthworm's middle section and then into a side corridor. "Follow me."

They made their way up a narrow staircase.

The size of the place still shocked Sarah. It could have housed a thousand employees, probably more, but a person could die inside the Earthworm and never be found with the way things were.

The long staircase wound back and forth on itself, a coiled python. By the time Sarah reached the top, she was sweating. Howard and Bradley were waiting for her there—two minutes ahead, subtle grins on their faces and their hands on their hips.

"You get used to it," said Bradley. "There was supposed to be a lift, but then..."

"Yeah, I know," said Sarah. "Funding. How is this place not falling apart? It's huge. And empty."

"Sergeant Mattock's strike team comes and goes, but we feel he's better placed out in the field. There used to be more of us once." He held open a door and daylight bled into the stairwell with a warm almost-summer breeze. Sarah smiled as she felt the breeze tickle her face. It felt good to get out of that pit and back out into the open air.

They emerged from inside a rickety shed onto a derelict farm. Sarah glanced around at the various outbuildings and empty livestock pens. A rusty tractor sat parked up against an old farmhouse, which was missing both its roof and one wall. Rocks and weeds jutted out of the ground where there may once have been crops.

"It's our disguise," said Bradley.

Sarah nodded. "It's a good one. I wouldn't want to go snooping around this place. It looks like Old MacDonald haunts it."

"It's more high-tech than it looks," said Howard. "There are cameras hidden in a dozen places." He pointed to the tractor, and Sarah saw the glint of a lens hidden inside the exhaust pipe.

She put her hands on her hips. "So, do you plan on walking to Oxford? Because I didn't wear the right shoes."

Howard trudged through the mud toward a listing feed shed. Its entrance was fitted with a collection of padlocks, but all of them had been popped open. Howard pulled open the sheet-metal doors to reveal Mandy standing inside. The big guy nodded at Howard and Bradley as they entered, but gave Sarah only a cursory glance.

"Good to see you again, too," she grunted.

Inside the feed shed, a group of powerful super bikes sat beside two sleek saloons. Near the front, two jet-black Range Rover Westminsters idled. The two 4x4s made Sarah think of the Snatch Land Rovers used in Afghanistan. She shuddered.

"You okay, Captain?" Bradley asked her.

"Fine. So these are our rides, huh? Not the latest models,

but pretty swank. Way things were downstairs, I was expecting a couple of Mini Metros."

Howard rolled his eyes. "We do the best we can with what we have. Didn't they teach you that in the Army?"

"No," said Sarah in a put-on dopey voice. "They just taught me which end of the rifle to point at the bad guys."

Howard opened the passenger door of one of the two Ranges and glanced over at the other one. "Bradley, you take second, follow me and Mandy."

Bradley hopped up into the other vehicle, silent and shaky. He looked like he was about to take a big test. *He isn't good in the field at all, is he?* Sarah noted.

Mandy gunned the engine and took off in the first Range Rover. Bradley waited for Sarah to get into the passenger seat, but she went around to the driver's side and elbowed him. "Shove over. I'm driving."

"But... Howard told me to—"

"Just move over," Sarah said. Bradley hopped across to the passenger seat, and Sarah shifted into first gear. The engine grumbled as she brought up the clutch. She revved the engine and took off after the other Range. It was already a quarter-mile ahead, so she stepped on it, flinging poor Bradley back in his seat. Within a couple of minutes, she was side-by-side with Howard's vehicle and doing north of a ton. It was a hell of a rush.

Bradley directed Sarah to a gate at the edge of the field. She slowed the Range abruptly, skidding to a halt.

Mandy parked the other Range beside her. Howard leapt out. "Do you think we're messing around here? We're trying to catch the people responsible for four terrorist attacks, and you're racing around like you're on *Top Gear*. I told Bradley to drive."

"He said he couldn't concentrate with me sitting next to

him. He wanted me to take the wheel so he was free to touch himself."

Bradley went bright red.

Howard sighed. "Look, I understand the whole attitude thing. It comes with the scar, I get it. But can I rely on you?"

The question made Sarah angry. "I can handle my shit. You handle yours."

"I'm taking lead. Follow me, and keep the Mario Kart shit to a minimum."

Sarah snapped off another mock salute. "Roger that."

They got moving and drove out of the gate, pausing while Bradley closed it behind them.

"What's Howard's deal?" Sarah asked Bradley after they had driven for a while in silence.

"What do you mean?"

"Why's he got such a stick up his arse?"

Bradley shrugged. "Just the way he is."

"Bad childhood?"

"Nope. Howard was an Assistant-Lecturer at Nottingham. He was teaching Terrorism and Security studies when MCU recruited him. When he was younger, he almost made it as a professional tennis player, but chose University. His father was a carpenter, and his mother stayed home. He has the least baggage out of everybody at MCU."

"What, all five of you?"

"There are more of us than that. Like I said earlier, we have a field team. Sergeant Mattock leads it. He's ex SAS."

Sarah's heart skipped a beat. Mattock was SAS, which meant he'd know her father. All SAS knew Major Stone. "Another thug with a beige beret, right?" she said. "Shoot first, ask questions later. I've met the type before."

Bradley looked out his window. "You'll be glad to have him if you need him. He's the only reason Howard didn't die when

I froze. It might be MCU's job to protect the country, but Mattock's job is to protect us."

"I don't need protecting."

"Good for you. The rest of us aren't perfect, so it's nice to have a little help when we can get it."

They sat in silence for the next twelve miles. The roads were quiet for a Monday afternoon. The latest terrorist tape had sent the country into hiding. People wouldn't leave their houses for fear of getting blown to pieces by maniacs. Sarah wondered how many people had left their jobs today after the latest video. The economy would already be suffering just hours after the attacks. No doubt the Stock Market had plummeted, as it was wont to do in times of crisis, just to add to the misery.

Howard spoke over the radio, breaking the silence. Sarah hadn't realised the Range Rovers were comm-linked. "I just got an update from Palu."

"Cartwright's receptionist said the doctor is with patients today. He's at his office. Mission to extract is green, but we need to go in soft. Our target is in place, but we can't afford to endanger civilians."

"Civilians are in danger every time they cross the street," Sarah said. "So what's the plan?"

"I'll go in alone and speak with the doctor. If I feel he has information on the attacks, I'll bring him in."

"Alone?" Bradley asked.

"I can take a civilian on my own easily enough, Bradley. If I need your help I'll give the signal. Keep your line open."

"Roger that," Bradley said.

Sarah folded her arms. "So, our orders are to sit in the car and do nothing? Not very James Bondy."

"Don't worry," Bradley said. "I play a mean eye-spy."

Sarah didn't know if the kid was joking.

10

WHO DARES WINS

They entered the city of Oxford forty minutes later, driving through the high street and cutting between the Norman, Gothic, and Victorian architecture that mingled with the grand buildings of the world's oldest English-speaking university. It was a city that cried 'England,' but at the same time, was undeniably cosmopolitan.

As Sarah moved through loose traffic, she spotted students of various nationalities talking, hugging, and crying as they no doubt discussed the day's terrible events. It was a microcosmic example of how the world could be when petty differences and culture were set aside. It almost restored Sarah's faith in humanity, until she remembered that Wazir Hesbani had also attended Oxford University. *How many of these kids will grow up to be monsters?*

Howard came over the radio. "The clinic is a half-mile from here," he said. "Stay close, but keep a little distance. When I park up, find a place nearby and wait for my signal. Mandy will be on standby in case I need to make an extraction. Bradley, you and Sarah are to remain in a support role."

"Roger that."

The radio went silent.

"The only thing with a support role in this car is my bra," said Sarah, making Bradley blush. "Any sign of trouble and I'll go get the doctor myself."

"We don't know the doctor had anything to do with the bombings."

"For his sake, I hope not."

Howard took a series of side streets that led into an office district. The buildings were modern and red-bricked, contrasting from the darker stone buildings of the city centre. Sarah followed behind until he pulled into a small car park in front of a three-story building. Sarah overshot the car park and came to a halt around the corner in front of a newsagent.

"I'm entering the building now," Howard said over the radio. "Stand by."

Sarah leaned forward and replied, "Roger that, ten-four, Captain Badger."

Howard didn't reply, but she heard him sigh before the radio cut off.

"Why do you like winding people up so much?" Bradley asked.

"I can't get laid. What else am I supposed to do for kicks?"

Bradley blushed, but he kept on at her. "Do you mean because of your scars? That puts men off?"

"What d'you think?"

Bradley shrugged. "I don't know. I imagine people would stop noticing after a while, but I don't think it's as much of a problem as you think. My little sister has *spina bifeda,* but she never lets it hold her back. She's happy. It's all about how you look at yourself, not how other people look at you."

"Your sister is unhappy, trust me. The brave face she puts on is just for you. She knows that if she feels sorry for herself, you'll all grow tired of her. Every time she smiles, she dies a little more inside, trying to make herself less of a burden to the rest of you. Your sister might be brave, but she's not happy."

"Screw you. You know nothing."

Sarah grinned. "There you go. Sooner you realise the world is less Disney and a lot more News at 10, the better."

Bradley stared out of his window in silence.

Sarah glanced around, checking out the area where they'd parked. It was a nice part of town. New buildings nestled between patches of grass and shade-giving trees. The type of place you'd expect to find a psychiatrist working, certainly not a terrorist.

Sarah noticed a girl working inside the newsagent who was staring at them. She talked on a phone while eyeing the Range Rover. Sarah and Bradley had broken no laws, just parked in the street. So why was this girl taking such an interest in them?

Something was off.

From the way the girl's vision fixed on the Range Rover, there was no way she was looking at anything else.

Sarah had suffered enough scrutiny for one day. She got out of the Range and climbed the single step into the newsagent's front door. Howard wouldn't like it, but she would be damned if she would sit and be stared at the whole time she was waiting.

When the girl saw her coming inside, she muttered something into the phone and hung up. She gave Sarah a wide, welcoming smile. "Hi, there. How are you today?"

"I'm fine. You okay with me parking out there?"

The girl seemed confused and unsettled. It might have been because of Sarah's scars. "No. No problem. You're welcome to park there."

Sarah strolled around the shop, glancing at stacks of newspapers as if they were the most interesting things in the world and taking her time. Eventually she turned back to the girl. "You here all by yourself, sweetheart?"

"I… yes, for the time being. Why do you ask?"

"I used to work in a shop like this," Sarah lied. "I remember how my boss used to leave me holding the fort all the time too. Sucks being all alone." She walked up to the counter and placed both hands on it.

The girl swallowed.

Sarah grinned, knowing that doing so would distort her gruesome face even further. "Try to mind your own business, sweetheart. I would hate if we were forced to become better acquainted."

Sarah left the newsagent and re-joined Bradley in the car.

"Everything okay?" he asked her.

"Something's off about the girl in that newsagent. Don't ask me why."

"You think she knows something?"

"Either that or she's just a nosey beggar. Most shop workers don't even give the time of day to customers standing in front of them, let alone a car parked outside on the road doing nothing. I'll give her the benefit of the doubt for now, but she's got my glands tickling. Heard anything from Howard?"

"Nope, all's quiet. Sorry." By Bradley's tone, it was clear he was still upset with her. When Sarah thought of what she'd said about his sister, she could understand why.

"Look, Bradley, I'm sorry—"

The radio squawked and Howard's voice rang out. "Target has flown the nest. Repeat: target is gone. Be on the lookout; he got wind we were coming. Suspect is a middle-aged man, spectacles, receding brown hair, shirt, tie, trousers."

"Somebody must have warned him," Bradley said.

"That bitch." Sarah leapt out of the Range and raced back into the newsagent. The girl was gone. A door in the back hung open. "I'm going to kick your skinny little ass," Sarah shouted. She bounded through the open door and found herself in a bricked yard, but there was no sign of the girl.

The sound of an engine.

Sarah saw the sky-blue Citroen speeding towards her and shouted "Stop," but without a gun, the demand was impotent. Yet, surprisingly, the driver stepped on the brake.

Sarah rushed to the driver's side door, snarling and shouting, but it was an old lady at the wheel. "Oh! S-sorry, ma'am, I thought you were a friend of mine."

The old lady spluttered, "That's how you treat your friends?" She sped off, no doubt wanting to get as far away from Sarah as she could. Sarah didn't blame her.

That ten-second delay could be all it took for the shop girl to get away, so Sarah got moving again. She heard racing footsteps ahead of her and went after them. She picked up speed, wishing she'd kept herself in better shape. The old wound in her thigh throbbed.

She rounded a corner and caught sight of her target. They were heading back around to the front of the newsagent. Ahead was the doctor's clinic, and Mandy, sitting in the other Range Rover. *She's making a play for the doctor*, thought Sarah. *I knew she was involved in something.*

Sarah tried to shout a warning to Mandy, but was too late. Her teammate was forced to duck down in his seat as the shop girl opened fire at him. Despite being unarmed, Sarah kept up her pursuit.

Mandy slipped out of the driver's side door and popped up over the hood to return fire from his own pistol, but the girl had him pinned, and his return shots were blind.

Bradley appeared, coming up the left and adding another

gun into the fray. Mandy held his cover on the right while Sarah rushed up the back.

The clinic's main entrance opened and Howard appeared from within. The girl had no place to go now, surrounded on all sides.

But when Howard exited the building, he was not alone. A man fitting Dr Cartwright's description was there also, and he had a syringe full of something pressed up against Howard's jugular. "L-let me out of h-here," he demanded, all three chins wobbling. "Let me out of here or I'll fill him full of enough diazepam to kill a herd of buffalo."

"Take the shot, Mandy!" Howard snarled. "He's got no place to go."

The shop girl fired at Mandy again and kept him pinned behind the Range. Sarah tried to come up behind the girl, but narrowly avoided getting a bullet in the temple. She skidded on her heels and put her hands up, wishing she'd asked for a gun before leaving the Earthworm.

Bradley stood in a firing position to the left, but was struggling to keep his aim straight. His face was pale and sweaty.

"Everybody chill the fuck out," said the shop girl. "Dr Cartwright, are you okay?"

The fat doctor nodded. "I-I took him by surprise. If you hadn't warned me, Ashley..."

The girl winced at the sound of her name being given away so cheaply. "You can thank me later. We have to get you out of here. Your skills are needed."

"Nobody's going anywhere," Howard said, defiant of the arm around his throat and the needle against his jugular.

"Excuse me, handsome," Ashley said, "but you're not in a position to negotiate. I'm the one with the testicles here."

Mandy tried to creep up and let off another shot, but Ashley aimed at him and shook her head to warn him. Sarah eyed Bradley and tried to signal at him to shoot. He had a bead on the girl's flank and could end this now, but he was frozen on the spot.

"What do you want?" Sarah asked the girl, stalling for a moment while Bradley searched for his balls. "Why are you working with terrorists?"

Ashley turned so that she could see Sarah, who was now standing just twelve feet behind her. "Honey, we *are* terrorists."

"We are no such thing," argued Dr Cartwright.

Ashley rolled her eyes. "Keep telling yourself that, Doc, but you knew there would be blood on your hands. You can't change the world with hypotheses. We've all taken a hand in what's happening. But don't worry so much, Doc. Today's terrorists are tomorrow's freedom fighters. Just look at Mandela. Future generations will thank us, even if this one doesn't."

"I want to get out of here," Dr Cartwright said.

Ashley switched her aim between Mandy, Bradley, and Sarah, then back again. "Doc, if anybody moves, inject that son-of-a-bitch with whatever it is you have there, understand me?"

"Yes."

Ashley slid between a pair of parked cars and fumbled in her jeans pocket with her free hand, keeping the gun raised with her other.

Sarah crept forward. Bradley followed her lead and got closer too—not that the kid would be any use if he couldn't pull the trigger.

Ashley thumbed a button on a key fob, and a blue Ford Focus flashed its lights. "Get in," she told the doctor.

"What about him?" The doctor was talking about Howard, still held hostage by his needle.

"He comes with us."

"No," said Sarah. "Hand him over, and we'll let you leave."

"I'm leaving anyway," said Ashley. "So keep your compromises to yourself, freak."

Sarah really wanted to kick the girl's ass now. *We'll see how pretty* she *is when I'm done with her.*

"Get in the car," Ashley ordered the doctor again.

Cartwright reached around Howard and pulled open the rear passenger door of the Ford. He then awkwardly began to shove and position Howard inside, but couldn't keep the needle in place while doing it.

Howard spun around on the back seat of the car, yanked the doctor down on top of him, and then head butted him in the face.

Cartwright slumped into the Ford's rear foot well and wailed like a wounded lamb. Howard leapt out of the car and rolled across the tarmac, throwing himself behind a Toyota minivan for cover.

Ashley opened fire. She missed Howard with her first two shots, then readjusted and fired the next two at Mandy just as he was about to pop up from cover.

Sarah saw her chance and rushed toward the girl from behind. She made it halfway before something stung her shoulder and dropped her to her knees. Her vision tilted, and she gritted her teeth as pain overwhelmed her.

Ashley fired another round, this one at Mandy, and then several more at Bradley. Sarah remained on her knees, wondering who the hell this girl was, and who had trained her.

Sarah slumped forward onto her hands, feeling like she was going to be sick. Ashley approached her, an animalistic expression on her face. She pointed the gun at Sarah's forehead. "You idiots have no idea what's happening, do you? We're going to bring this whole country to its knees. Too bad

I'm going to put you out of your misery before you have chance to see it."

Sarah closed her eyes and waited for the sound of the gunshot that would end her life. She had expected death so many times before that she was a little glad it was finally here.

Blam!

Sarah flew backwards, but it was out of fright, not pain or impact. She opened her eyes and found Ashley clutching her right hand and cursing. Blood spewed from the girl's fingertips. Her gun lay several feet away on the concrete.

Bradley took another shot, but this one missed. Ashley leapt out of the way and sprinted for the Ford. Mandy let off several shots at her as she leapt in behind the steering wheel, but his clip ran dry and he was forced to reload.

Ashley kicked close the rear door of the car, trapping Dr Cartwright inside, and then slid behind the steering wheel. She was out of the car park and around the corner before the rest of them had chance to recover. Rather than chase their target, Howard, Bradley, and Mandy rushed over to Sarah. Bradley knelt beside her and pressed his hand hard against her shoulder. It hurt like hell and made her eyes roll back in her head.

"You've been shot," said Bradley, "but you're going to be okay. We're going to get you help."

"It's my fault," Howard said. "I let the doctor get a jump on me."

"You're letting her get away," Sarah said, feeling herself fading.

Howard stroked her hair. "She's already gone. This whole thing has been a bust. Mandy, get Sarah to the Range Rover, we need to get her back to Dr Bennett."

Sarah felt herself lifted into the air by a giant and then closed her eyes to dream.

11

THE BLUE PILL

AFGHANISTAN, 2008

When Sarah opened her eyes, sweating stone surrounded her on all sides, and the sun scorched through a narrow opening near the ceiling. It was like waking up inside a kiln.

There was a wooden door at one end of the room and Sarah crawled over to it. Dirt and stone bit at her palms and her right leg dragged behind her, numb and heavy. When she reached the door she pulled herself halfway up it and shouted, "Let me out of here!"

But no one came to help her. She knew nobody would, but something human inside of her wouldn't allow her to just sit there and rot.

Her face was on fire. A bandage covered her right leg, but her face was raw as she brushed it with her fingertips. Every touch was broken glass beneath her skin and brought tears to her eyes.

She beat her fists against the wooden door, but it barely moved. It was ancient and thick, cut from a tree likely a

The entire day had been something out of a contrived thriller novel. It was as if the ghosts of Sarah's past had teamed up to haunt her all at once: Hesbani, Al-Sharir... her father. And somehow she knew things were only going to get worse.

Sarah lowered her speed—not in such a hurry anymore.

hundred years dead. There was nothing of any use inside her pockets; they'd taken everything from her, even her dog tags.

Sarah thought about her father and how ashamed he would be of her. Being captured was worse than death, in his eyes. Better to eat your own bullet than let the enemy take you. The SAS did not get captured—ever. If the enemy caught you, it was because you'd stopped fighting, and when you stopped fighting, you deserved everything you got.

Thomas was the one who worried her most. What would he do when he heard she'd been captured? If they buried her in the desert, would he ever know for sure she was dead? Would he spend the rest of his life wondering? Wondering about the child she was carrying?

Sarah couldn't help herself, she wept. Her legs spread out in the dirt, and she slumped against the wall, hating herself for being so weak. She was alone, and it was awful, but she knew that when company arrived, things would get even worse. Torture and death awaited her. The best she could hope for was that her body found its way home.

She thought of her men: Hamish, Miller, and the young privates she'd never gotten to know. Were they all dead, or had they been taken prisoner? She couldn't believe how badly she'd failed them. Their lives had been in her hands, and she'd let them down.

"Just kill me," she shouted. "You hear me? I have nothing to give you, so just kill me and be done with it."

The wooden door opened, and a man stepped inside. Middle-aged, he wore full Pashtun dress with a *Taqiyah*, a short, rounded skullcap. He smiled at her in the glow of the doorway, and for a moment, he looked angelic. "If I wish for you to be dead, Captain, then dead you would be."

Wazir Hesbani, the one who'd burned her face with gunpowder, stood behind the new man, glaring at her. Like

Hesbani, the new man had a tattoo of a dagger on his forearm.

Sarah shuffled in the dirt, away from the two men.

"Relax. I bring only bread and water," said the unknown man, "and a willingness to chat."

"I won't tell you anything." Sarah tried to speak firmly, but her voice quivered.

"That is up to you, Captain. I am not here to force you to do anything. You are my guest."

"Then let me go."

"In time."

"What do you want?"

"To chat."

"My mission was to speak with a village elder," she said, tight-lipped. "That is the only intel I have, and you should know because everything that happened in the village was all a trap. You were no doubt behind it."

The man placed the tray on the floor. "The elder you came to speak to is dead. Taliban took the village many days ago, and your Army didn't even know it. What happen today was due to your own failings. It is your own weakness that has allowing your enemy to best you."

Sarah was confused. "Are you not Taliban?"

"My name is Al Al-Sharir, and I am just a man, born in Afghanistan, a Muslim. I make no choice to be here instead of there, or to be Muslim instead of Christian. It is just what I am. I am no Taliban, but neither am I their enemy. Taliban just one group of many that fight for what they believing is right. You fight for what you believing is right, yes?"

Sarah nodded.

"Then you are no different than Taliban. A coin is having two sides, but both equal, yes? Your right does not make other rights wrong."

Sarah struggled to understand. "What do *you* believe is right?"

Al-Sharir smiled. "That all of us are wrong and that there is no right." He held up his wrist to show her the tattoo of the dagger.

Sarah shook her head in confusion.

"It is symbol, that my will belong to Allah. There is no place for my own selfish desires. My life is on the tip of a dagger and I can die any second. Allah allows life, and only he has right to take it. We are not here to rule in his place."

"We're just trying to help you people."

"Then why enter our country after events of 9/11? Is not anger and fear which bring you here, no? What is it about now that makes your assistance necessary? Do not fool yourself, Captain, you are uninvited guests."

"But by killing us, you're just keep us here longer. Where is the sense in that?"

"I make sense of the world in my own small way, as must we all."

Sarah felt more tears spill down her cheeks, stinging her wounds. "P-please, let me go," she begged.

Al-Sharir sighed. "I will send you back, yes, but I am afraid I must first do what you expect me to do."

Sarah's heart beat against her ribs. "You're going to torture me."

"Not me, but someone, yes. We must do unto you as you do unto others. It is the only lesson we have to teach here. My friend, Wazir, is a keen teacher. He will prefer you do not talk easily."

Sarah could sense Wazir lingering in the doorway. When she looked, his eyes were still set on her, staring hungrily. "I-I don't know anything. You sound like a good man, Al-Sharir. You don't have to do this."

"I am no good man. We must stop thinking in such flimsy ideals such as good and bad." He reached for Sarah, grabbed the thumb of her left hand and twisted.

Sarah screamed as her knuckle dislocated, and fire shot up her entire arm. She tried to speak, but couldn't catch her breath, so she sobbed like a child.

Al-Sharir sighed. "I am no good man. If you were an innocent woman, I would let you go home, but you are no innocent woman. You are a soldier. You are willing to take life, so you must be willing to give it." He pointed to the dagger tattoo on his arm. "The dagger points towards my heart because I am willing to die for what is right. That badge on your uniform is your dagger. It say you are willing to die for your beliefs as I am for mine."

Sarah looked at the captain's bands on her dirty uniform and wept, but she managed to splutter out one final plea for mercy. "I'm pregnant."

Al-Sharir's eyes flickered as he studied her face. "You speak lies. A clever way for you to beg of me, but it is game I will not play."

Sarah grabbed the man by his wrist. "I swear to you, I'm pregnant. I don't want to be a soldier anymore, I want to be a mother."

Al-Sharir stared at her for what felt like an eternity. Eventually he nodded. "I cannot harm the innocent inside of you, so I shall release you in the morning. If you are lying, your punishment will be great and everlasting."

Sarah's eyes flooded as she nodded. "Thank you," she said. "Thank you. I'm not lying, I promise."

"I hope not." Al-Sharir rose to his feet. "Because if I have judged you wrong in this life, Allah will correct my mistake in the next. I will see you again in the morning. Until then, you will have company."

Al-Sharir headed for the door. As he did, Hesbani stalked toward Sarah. "No," she said, "you said you wouldn't let him have me. I'm carrying a baby!"

Hesbani sneered at her. "Don't worry, English. I will not hurt you. I am tired after spending so long with your friend."

Sarah frowned. "My friend? What–"

Hesbani booted Sarah in the face, cutting off her words and splitting both her lips wide open.

"You do not speak, English."

Hesbani spat at her before he walked away and left the room. Two other men entered and threw a body to the ground beside Sarah. When the wooden door closed, leaving her in near darkness, Sarah realised the man was beaten and semi-conscious—and a British soldier. He looked up at her with swollen, bruised eyes and tried to talk, but could only wheeze.

Sarah shuffled until she was close enough to cradle the injured man in her arms. She felt more tears spill from her eyes as she realised who it was. "Hamish," she said, through her swollen, bleeding lips. "What have they done to you?"

MCU, ENGLISH COUNTRYSIDE, 2014

Sarah let out a moan as past miseries jolted her awake. She tried to move, but couldn't. Her body floated through the air, her legs dangling. At first she couldn't hear anything, but then it all came rushing back.

Mandy glanced at Sarah as he carried her, his face pained and beads of sweat running down his nose. Sarah didn't mind being carried. She felt safe, like a baby.

Fluorescent lights hummed on the ceiling above her, hurting her eyes. The smell of chemicals bleached the air.

"Put her down on the table, quickly!"

Sarah was placed down on something hard. Her legs

straightened, and her head lolled to one side. Dr Bennett looked at her and placed a hand on her cheek. "You're going to be just fine, Sarah. You're back at MCU. You've been shot, but I'm handling it. Lie back and relax."

Sarah lay still. There was a subtle pinch at her wrist followed by a tugging sensation.

"How long ago did this happen?" Bennett asked someone else in the room.

Howard answered. "Thirty minutes ago. I kept pressure on the wound, but she lost a lot of blood."

Bennett hissed. "You should have called an ambulance."

"We're not supposed to advertise our existence, remember?"

"I don't give a damn. You risked her life bringing her all the way back here."

Sarah felt light-headed and wanted to tell them to stop bickering, but no words would come. Her eyelids drooped, and she couldn't feel her face. Even the pain of her scars had gone.

"Sarah, I've given you a painkiller," said Bennett. "You're going to feel very sleepy. Don't fight it. You will be fine."

Sarah closed her eyes.

When she opened them again, she was tucked beneath several sheets. She tried to sit up, but grunted from the pain and lay back. Her shoulder ached, and she could feel a thick bandage beneath her chin. She was in pain, but that was nothing new. Not a minute passed without her face throbbing and burning; the wound in her shoulder just added a little variety. Her most pressing concern was that she was stark-bollock-naked beneath the sheets.

It was then that Sarah spotted the small red button attached to a wire. She thumbed it several times and hoped an irritating alarm was sounding somewhere. Sure enough, Dr Bennett entered the room a minute later.

"Sarah," she said, "you're awake. How are you feeling? Any pain?"

"Not too much. How long have I been out?"

"Eight hours. You're still under sedation so you might feel peculiar for a while. The bullet lodged beneath your collar-bone. You have a small fracture and some tissue damage. Lost a couple pints of blood too, but nothing you won't get back. You need to rest."

As the doctor spoke, Sarah's vision tilted back and forth. "I feel light-headed. You sure it was only two pints?"

Bennett smiled. "A tad more perhaps, but you're going to be just fine. Like I said, you need rest."

Sarah slid her legs over the bed's rail and her bare feet slapped the floor. She stood in front of Dr Bennett naked. "No can do, Doc. I'm not the bed-rest type. Where are my clothes?"

The door at the back of the room opened, and Bradley entered. He saw Sarah naked and skidded on his heels, putting his hands over his face and turning around. "Jesus, Captain, I'm sorry. I came to get Dr Bennett."

Sarah remained standing. She wasn't shy about her body. With a face like hers, dignity went out the window. "Don't worry," she purred. "I thought you were here for the magazine shoot."

Bradley couldn't face her. "You should put some clothes on."

"Nah, I'm good."

Howard entered the room next. He saw Sarah standing naked and acted exactly as Bradley had. Now he and Bradley stood side-by-side with their backs to her, covering their eyes. "Sarah, I'm sorry. I came to check on you."

Dr Bennett rolled her eyes. "Captain Stone, there are

clothes for you in the wardrobe. Perhaps you should put them on if you insist on staying out of bed."

Sarah headed for the wardrobe and tried to hide the weakness in her legs. It felt like she'd run a marathon, followed by a mountain hike, followed by a pie-eating contest. She struggled to breathe, but made it to the wardrobe and found a pressed black suit inside.

"It's one of mine," said Bennett, "but you're welcome to have it."

Sarah pulled the clothes on gingerly and buttoned up the shirt with clumsy hands. When she bent to lace her shoes, she went crashing to the floor.

Bradley and Howard rushed to her aid. Dr Bennett folded her arms and tapped her foot. "I told you, you need rest."

Bradley helped Sarah tie her shoelaces, while Howard propped her up and said, "You okay, champ?"

She frowned. "You're going with 'champ', huh?"

Howard smirked. "You able to get up, Grumpy Tits? Is that better?"

Sarah nodded. She placed a hand on Howard's shoulder, and he helped her to her feet.

"What did you want me for?" Dr Bennett asked Bradley.

"Oh," he said. "Director Palu wants all of us in the conference room. We've found out who the girl at the clinic was. Palu wants to track her down ASAP."

"Yeah, me too," Sarah said, "so I can kick her arse."

Howard patted her on the back. "You'll get your chance, Champ. I promise."

Sarah tried to pretend the pat on her back didn't nearly floor her.

12

DOWN THE RABBIT HOLE

Sarah eased herself into a chair at the conference table. When Sarah checked her watch, it was 2:30 in the morning.

Palu was weary and pale. "Hello, Captain Stone," he said, eyeing her change of clothes. He had also changed. The yellow shirt had given way to a sombre pink. "I'm relieved to know you're okay. The last thing we need right now is the red tape that surrounds the death of a team member."

"I didn't know you cared."

"I have advised the patient to remain in bed," Dr Bennett said. "Let it be noted that she refused."

"Noted," Palu said. "Now, can we please get to business?"

"What do we have?" Bradley asked.

Palu opened a laptop and clicked through files while giving them preliminary intel. "I had the Home Office run employment checks on the newsagent. I was surprised to find that the suspect who snatched Dr Cartwright was officially employed there. There are National Insurance records and Income Tax reports... It's almost like she didn't care about being found."

"Or she never expected anyone to look for her," said Sarah.

"Her name is Ashley Foster," Palu continued. "We have her address, educational and employment background, medical history, pretty much everything. She seems like an ordinary teenage girl, on the surface."

Sarah folded her arms and winced at the pain in her shoulder. "An ordinary teenage girl doesn't throw her life away, firing guns at... who are we exactly? I want to say the Justice League."

"We are the Major Crimes Unit," Palu stated, "and we take our job very seriously. If being shot hasn't taught you what we're up against, Captain, then I have no idea what will." There was an uncomfortable silence for a moment as he brought new information up on the big screen—a photograph of the girl who had shot Sarah. "Ashley Foster drifted between part-time jobs, until nine months ago, when she started working at the newsagent opposite Cartwright's office. We don't know who she's been associating with or what her connection is to the doctor. The newsagent is registered to a Pakistani immigrant who's currently out of the country. His niece, Aziza Hamidi, is running things in his absence, but the address we found for her is old. Background checks we ran all came up blank."

"So we need to know how Ashley Foster knows Dr Cartwright," said Howard. "Was she in therapy?"

"Not that I can tell," Palu answered. "Her medical records are thin. There's no reason to believe she is anything other than a healthy teenager, if not for today's events."

"One thing that psycho-diva is not," snarled Sarah, "is healthy minded. She was running and gunning like a Spetnaz on Smarties. The only thing that makes a person behave that way is a death wish. Ashley Foster has some serious issues, I promise you."

"Her actions certainly warrant extreme caution," Bennett agreed, much to Sarah's surprise.

"We need to find out what her motives are," said Palu. "We have the address of her parents and should go talk to them, see if they know anything about their daughter's involvement in yesterday's events."

Sarah went to get up from the table.

Howard frowned at her. "Where do you think you're going? I'll handle this, you're still healing."

Sarah ignored him and stood up anyway. "I'm fine. And do you mean 'handle it' like you did at the clinic? You became a hostage."

Howard glowered at her from across the table. "I admit that was a major screw up, but if we didn't have to tend to an injured teammate, we could have pursued the target."

"That's a little unfair," said Bradley. "Sarah was unarmed, and Ashley Foster escaped before we even had chance to pursue."

"*You* weren't unarmed though," said Howard to Bradley. "You should've taken your shot earlier."

"Enough," said Palu. "Dr Bennett, is Captain Stone fit to resume active duty?"

Bennett sniffed. "Not even close. She's still partially sedated, and her body needs to replace the blood it lost."

"Am I in any danger?" Sarah asked. "Beyond passing out or accidentally farting?"

Dr Bennett folded her arms and shrugged. "Your stitches could open, and you might go into shock if you lose more blood. But, I suppose, if you take it easy, you may get away with just feeling like you're eighty years old. Good enough reason for you to stay put if you ask me."

"I'm going," said Sarah. "I'm the one Ashley Foster shot, and I would like to know who raised her to be a cross between

Norman Bates and Rambo. This girl has training. I don't think we should take her for granted."

"This is not a mission of force," said Palu. "We just need to speak with the family before we make any snap decisions. If you have a grudge, you should let Howard take this one alone. The family will feel threatened enough as it is, without having a mob turning up on their doorstep in the early hours."

Sarah sighed. "You're right, it's not the right call to go in heavy. But sending me in with Howard is the right call. Not only am I a woman, which has its own benefits, but I'm also a trained interrogator. In the Army, I was a liaison for local tribes and villagers. I'm trained to get answers from people who don't want to give them."

"Are you saying you tortured people?" asked Bradley, his eyes widening.

Sarah shook her head. "No torture. I have a built-in bullshit detector. If a person is hiding something, I can tell."

Howard glanced at Palu and shrugged. "It's true. Part of the reason I brought her in was because of her interrogation training. None of us have that."

"And her 'bullshit-detector' is exactly what she used earlier with the staged videotape," said Bradley. "None of us picked up any of those clues."

Sarah thought about how her skills weren't as great as her MOD file probably made out. After all, it had only taken a woman and some watermelons to fool her. She compensated for her doubt with a joke. "It was those same skills that led me to figuring out that Howard is gay. Not that there's anything wrong with that. I just don't know why he tries so hard to hide it. We're all here for you, Howie."

Howard rolled his eyes and chuckled. He was starting to get her humour.

Palu waved a hand. "Okay fine, go, but I want no violence.

The parents are innocent civilians until we know different. It's their daughter we're after in the middle of the night, so show a little diplomacy."

"Hey, diplomatic is my middle name," Sarah said.

"Follow me," Howard told her. "We need to make a few stops before we set off."

Sarah frowned. "We should make a move."

Howard nodded but kept walking. "If you want my advice, I think you should get back in bed, but if you're determined to come with me, I would rather you have a weapon this time. We might run into Ashley Foster again. Sound good?"

Sarah grinned from ear to ear. "Show me the money."

Howard showed her the money. The MCU's armoury was a bank vault nestled inside the Earthworm's head behind a mundane steel door.

"Yikes! You have enough hardware here to kit out an army." Sarah gawped at the equipment on endless benches and shelves. It was a veritable museum of assault rifles, handguns, and other tactical weapons. Rows upon rows of Glock 9mms and Colt 45s, and many other side-arms. What surprised her most was a nest of military assault rifles lined up against the far wall. "Is that a FAMAS?" she asked, jaw agape.

"Yes."

"British forces don't use French assault rifles. How did you get it?"

Howard tapped a finger against his nose. "Special consignment. The MCU can use whatever hardware it feels is right for the situation. Originally, we were going to operate internationally—similar to the CIA and MI6—but things never progressed that far. We still have a mandate that allows us to use heavy force if necessary."

Sarah took one last look at the weaponry and let out a

whistle. She even spotted an F2000, which looked like something out of a sci-fi movie.

"Small arms only on this ride," Howard told her. "Grab yourself something comfortable."

Sarah went to the handgun rack and perused her choices. She saw Brownings and American Smith and Wessons, Walther PPKs, and various Glocks, as well as the ever popular Colt .45 and the M1911 (the 'Yankee Fist'), but her eyes were drawn to a SIG-Sauer P229. It was smaller and lighter than most of the other handguns. It was also similar to the side-arm she used on her tours of Afghanistan. Seeing one now made her skin prickle, and for a moment, the heat of the Middle-Eastern sun was on the back of her neck all over again. The nostalgia went away as soon as she placed her finger around the trigger. She'd convinced herself that the battle had been lost in Afghanistan, that the bad guys had beaten her, but the last twenty-four hours had shown her that the war was still going on, and that it was being fought at home as well as abroad. She was still a soldier, and she had a duty to do.

"The SIG?" Howard said. "Not bad, but I prefer something a little more robust."

Sarah blew a raspberry with her cheeks. "If you pick up a Desert Eagle or a Magnum, I will assume you have a tiny penis."

Howard smirked. He picked up a two-tone, silver handgun that was not a great deal bigger than her SIG, but unlike the stainless steel of her weapon, Howard's gun was a mix of Aluminium and polymer. "Ruger P95 Double Action," he explained. "Just feels good."

"I was the same way picking my vibrator," said Sarah. "I liked the cocking action of the Bushmaster 3000."

Howard blushed. Sarah betrayed her deadpan exterior and let a chuckle slip out. Howard had such a stick up his arse that it was too much fun rattling his cage. Somewhere deep inside, this guy with the jutting chin and perfectly shaved sideburns was just dying to let loose and enjoy himself.

Howard put on his grey woolen jacket and immediately a phone in his pocket rang. He pulled out his mob-sat and looked at Sarah. "Palu just sent us the Foster's address. You ready to head out?"

Sarah grabbed a waist holster and nodded. "Are we meeting Mandy up top?"

"Yeah. You'll rarely find him anyplace else."

Sarah thought about how Mandy had carried her through the Earthworm, and how concerned he had looked. It was a strange turn of events, considering how the giant had barely even grunted at her until then. "You know," she said, "you're going to have to tell me how he made that helicopter disappear yesterday. I don't imagine he left it in the middle of the field."

"And you'd be right," said Howard. "I'm sure Mandy will let you in on the secret if you ask him."

"He does talk, then?"

"Sometimes."

"What's his story? How is he such a good pilot? I don't think he's ex RAF."

"He's not," said Howard. "He's never been in any of the forces. He's a civilian. Paid for flight lessons himself. He was married once, but you'll have to ask *him* about it."

Sarah said no more as they headed up the same staircase they'd used before, the one that exited into the derelict farm.

Night had long fallen, making the abandoned sheds and agricultural equipment even more haunting. Gaps in the crumbling brickwork whistled as a breeze passed through them and owls hooted in the rotten eaves of the old buildings.

Sarah hugged herself and shivered, despite not feeling particularly cold.

They hurried to the warehouse where, sure enough, Mandy was waiting for them. The Range Rovers were parked near the back of the shed now, one of them pockmarked with bullet holes. “Best take one of the saloons,” said Howard. “If Ashley Foster warned her parents, they might be on the lookout for Range Rovers.”

Mandy grunted at them and fumbled in the pockets of his cargo pants, pulling out the correct set of keys. They unlocked a 2010 Jaguar XFR. Nothing too flashy, but far more luxurious than what Sarah was used to riding in. Before the MCU fell into disrepair, it’d clearly been given money to burn.

Mandy held open the Jaguar’s rear door for Sarah. She considered asking to drive, but knew she couldn’t shove Mandy aside like she had Bradley.

Howard sat up front. Sarah didn’t appreciate being dumped in the back, but for once, she didn’t complain. Her shoulder was throbbing, and her head had been fuzzy ever since waking. While she still had her wits about her, it took a concerted effort not to keel over and start panting. She hoped she could have a short rest on the drive to their destination.

The address Palu had given them was back in Oxford. Mandy started the engine and headed into the fields. Every jolt from the saloon’s suspension caused the pain in Sarah’s shoulder to flare. She hid it best she could.

“Do the parents know we’re coming?” she asked.

“No,” Howard said. “Unless Ashley warned them. We’ll play things cautiously. Mattock will be in the area ready to provide backup if needed.”

Sarah swallowed. “The SAS guy?”

Howard nodded. “Bradley must have told you about him.

He's a good guy to have in a pinch, no nonsense. You should like him."

I doubt it. "So, what type of background do the parents have? Any extreme political views?"

"Both are conservatives, but we'll try not to hold that against them."

Mandy snorted in the driver's seat.

Sarah frowned. "Don't you take orders from our conservative Prime Minister?"

"Yes," Howard said, "until the next one comes to power. Tell you the truth, I see little difference between any of the parties anymore. They used to stand for something, but it's all just a muddle now."

"There's something we can agree on," Sarah said.

They took ten minutes to enter the main roads. The Jaguar wasn't built for off-roading like the Range Rovers. Sarah clenched her jaw and thought about what she would do when she got hold of the people responsible for the attacks. The SIG attached to her belt was digging into her hip; she worried because of how much she liked the feel of it. If she looked like a monster, she saw little reason not to act like one. She wasn't going to be the only one with scars when this was over.

13

JACKED IN

When they reached the Foster's home, it was 4.30AM. The sky had turned a light shade of blue as the sun prepared to make its return. There was a chill to the air that made Sarah wonder if it was the weather or the fact she was a few pints short of blood.

Howard and Mandy had been silent the whole journey, and both seemed tired. She wondered how she looked herself.

The houses leading up to the Foster's address were a mixture of detached and semi-detached properties, with short lawns and well-kept bushes. Mandy pulled up outside of a double-fronted family home and blocked the property's driveway. A sleek, black Audi sat in front of the house next to a Mini Cooper. Both cars looked new.

Sarah pressed her forehead against the rear window and squinted. "Doesn't exactly look like Ashley had a troubled upbringing."

Howard shrugged. "Nobody knows what goes on behind closed doors. You ready?"

"What's the plan? Do we have fake Police badges or something?"

"You've been watching too many movies. We don't have specific identification, but most people don't tend to ask. Just speak with authority, and people will do what you say. If we need to, we can have Palu arrange for the local police to support us, but that's not how we want to do this."

"Okay, I'll follow your lead." Sarah pulled open her door and stepped onto the driveway.

"I'll take point," Howard said.

Sarah didn't argue. In the state she was in, she wasn't sure she could take charge even if she wanted to. They strolled up the driveway and approached the front door. A wall lantern switched on as they neared. Howard rang the bell. He rang it twice more before the hallway light came on.

The front door opened, and they were met by a bleary-eyed man in his fifties, fully dressed, despite the hour. "Have you found her?" he asked.

Howard frowned. "I'm sorry?"

The man looked at them like they were idiots. "My daughter, Ashley. Have you found her? You're the police, I take it?"

"No, we're not the police. We're special investigators for the Home Office."

Mr Foster nodded. "Oh, well, the police came by earlier. They said our daughter was involved in a kidnapping."

"That's right," said Howard. "A Dr Cartwright was also involved. Do you know him?"

Mr Foster shook his head.

"We'd like to come in for a chat, if that's okay," said Howard. "We'd very much like to locate your daughter, as I'm sure you would."

"Yes, please, of course." Mr Foster stood aside and allowed them into the hallway. His wife was coming down the stairs as they entered. She was wearing a dressing gown and rubbing at her eyes. Sarah noted the woman's eye make-up.

Howard nodded to the woman. “Ma’am.”

“They’ve come about Ashley,” Mr Foster told his wife.

Her eyes lit up. “Come into the kitchen; I’ll put some tea on.”

They headed down the hallway and entered a kitchen at the back of the house. The floor was a deep brown wood and the units were solid oak. Granite work surfaces and an expansive centre island completed the extravagant look, making it clear that the Foster family were doing all right for themselves.

“You have a lovely home,” said Sarah.

“Thank you,” Mrs Foster said. She glanced at Sarah and struggled to look away.

“You’re looking at my scars?”

“Sorry.”

“It’s okay. I served in Afghanistan. I left part of me over there.”

“Sorry.”

“Don’t be. I’m here to talk about your daughter, not my troubles.”

“I hope you don’t mind us waking you so early, Mr and Mrs Foster,” Howard said.

Mrs Foster smiled. “Please, call us Leanne and Paul. We just want to know our daughter is safe.”

“Okay,” Howard said, taking a seat. “Leanne, Paul, what do you know about what’s happened? Are you certain you don’t know Dr Cartwright?”

Leanne set two mugs of steaming tea on the counter and sat opposite Howard. “I don’t know anything,” she said. “Ashley went to work this morning as normal. Next thing we know, the police are contacting us, claiming our daughter is wanted in connection with a kidnapping and possible shooting. They wouldn’t tell us anything else. It’s insane.”

Paul hugged his wife. “I’m sure everything will work out, sweetheart. None of this makes any sense. There has to be an explanation.”

Howard smiled, then waited a while until the couple composed themselves. “Can you tell us about your daughter? Has she had any kind of problems that you know of?”

“No. Ashley wouldn’t hurt a fly.”

Sarah folded her arms and felt her shoulder throb. Yeah right.

“She hasn’t been in therapy?” Howard enquired. “Or in any kind of trouble with the courts? Sorry for having to ask such questions.”

Paul frowned. “No, she’s had no problems at all. She’s just a normal teenage girl. What do you think my daughter has done? What the police are saying must be a mistake. She would never kidnap anyone, she’s just a girl.”

“You’re right,” said Sarah. “She didn’t kidnap anybody. She helped a man escape. A man connected to the recent bombings.”

The faces of each parent dropped. It was Leanne who spoke. “There’s no way our daughter could be involved in that. No way. Who are you people? If you’re not the police...”

Howard sipped his tea and allowed a silence to settle over the room before he spoke. “We work for an agency committed to stopping terrorist threats against this nation. Your daughter is involved with a man linked to the recent bombings.”

Paul rubbed at his eyes. “Our daughter is innocent. I don’t know what she’s mixed up in, but she’s a sweet girl.”

“I believe you,” Howard said. “She’s too young to have done anything so wrong. I believe she’s gotten mixed up in something she doesn’t understand. All I want is to find her and help her. To do that I need to know all I can about her. Has she been acting strangely, out of character?”

Paul shook his head, but Leanne nodded. "She's been out a lot. I assumed she was seeing somebody." Her eyes went wide as if something occurred to her. "Maybe that's it. Maybe this psychiatrist, Dr Cartwright, has seduced our daughter and gotten her involved in something. Headshrinks know all kinds of ways to manipulate a person, don't they? It makes perfect sense."

Howard exchanged a knowing glance with Sarah. "Perhaps you're right," he said. "Do you have any idea where Ashley could be? The slightest guess."

"No idea," Leanne said.

Howard looked at Paul. "Me either," the man said. "I don't know where Ashley likes to go, other than work."

"Do you know who her boss is?" Howard asked.

Paul shook his head. "I've met the woman once or twice when I've stopped by the newsagent. Asian lady, has an accent. Whenever I see her she's all covered up, in those dresses they wear. You know?"

Howard nodded. "We're trying to track her down. Does Aziza Hamidi sound familiar?"

"All I know is that my daughter refers to her as 'Zee.'"

"Thank you," Howard said. "Is there anything else you can think of that might help us locate your daughter? Any friends she likes to visit, some place she might go if she were in trouble?"

"She'd come here," Leanne spluttered. "This is her home."

Howard looked at Sarah. "Anything you'd like to add, Sarah?"

"Just two things. The first question I have for Leanne and Paul is: why have you not asked what we know about your daughter? The normal reaction to have when we arrived would be to ask if we knew anything at all about Ashley. Whether she's safe, if there've been any sightings of her, that sort of thing. A parent should want to know everything they can, but the two of you have hardly asked anything. Your only concern has been telling us that your daughter is innocent. Neither of you have made eye-contact with one another either, which suggests you both have a story and are sticking to it. Often, people glance at one another for visual cues, but you both seem to be on the same page about this. And your mascara, Leanne: it's been on for a while, but none of it has smudged. Have you not been crying over what's happened today? Isn't Ashley your baby?"

"She is," cried Leanne, "and we want to know if she's okay. I assumed you would tell us if you knew anything. This is outrageous."

Paul folded his arms. "How dare you."

"Okay," Sarah said. "Perhaps I'm wrong. If so, I apologise. The other question I wanted to ask, is: how do you know Dr Cartwright is a psychiatrist? We never said so. We told you he was a doctor."

"The police told us," Paul said.

Sarah frowned. "But your wife said that the police gave no details other than that Ashley is wanted in connection with a kidnapping."

Howard nodded. "I know the police. They wouldn't have shared any information about the suspects. They wouldn't have mentioned anything specific concerning Dr Cartwright."

"The man works opposite our daughter in that clinic. It wasn't a massive assumption to make."

"No," Sarah said. "You said he was a psychiatrist specifically. The clinic across the road has half a dozen different specialists and a GP's office. It could make sense for you to guess Cartwright was a doctor, but not specifically that he's a therapist."

Leanne shifted in her seat. "Perhaps I have met Dr

Cartwright before and just can't remember. Come to think of it, Ashley might have gone out for a drink with him one time."

Sarah nodded. "That explains it then. Well, I guess we should get going, we need to find your daughter."

Paul smiled and took a swig of his tea. Leanne stood up from the breakfast bar. "Please, it's early. Let me grab you some breakfast for the road."

Sarah frowned. She'd gotten the feeling that the Fosters wanted she and Howard gone, but now they were being offered breakfast.

"That's quite alright," said Howard.

"At least have some fruit," Leanne insisted. She reached toward the middle of the counter where a wooden bowl of apples and bananas sat.

"Stop," said Sarah. "We're fine."

Leanne turned back and smiled. "I won't hear of it." She picked up an apple, which she fumbled to the floor. "Silly me, could one of you pick that up for me?"

Howard bent to pick the bruised apple up off the tiles.

Sarah shouted, "Howard, get down!" She slid the SIG from its holster and pointed it at Leanne Foster.

Leanne delved into the fruit bowl, just as Paul slipped from his stool and kneed the bent-over Howard in the face.

Howard hit the floor.

Leanne pulled a gun from the bottom of the fruit bowl. Pointed it. Squeezed the trigger.

Sarah fired first.

The first bullet struck Leanne in the shoulder, the following two, the chest. The woman cartwheeled backwards, dead before she hit the ground.

Paul saw his dead wife and howled in anguish. He charged at Sarah, but she was ready for him. Forgetting how weak and weary she was, she leapt aside and round kicked him in the belly. Paul wheezed, flailed, and then came at her again. Sarah smashed the butt of her SIG against his temple and dropped him to his knees.

"Lie down on the ground!" she shouted.

Paul Foster snarled. "You bitch."

Sarah snarled right back. "I'm the worst bitch from your worst nightmare, so don't even blink if you want to keep your teeth."

Howard clambered back to his feet, clutching his right eye. He moaned. "I'm hurt."

Sarah rolled her eyes. "Don't worry about it. At least your face will go back to normal. No hope for mine."

Howard smirked and reached into his jacket. He pulled out his mob-sat and dialed. "Mattock. I need an extraction—"

Blam!

Sarah ducked as gunfire took over the kitchen. Coming at them from the back of the room was Ashley Foster, running and gunning like she had outside the clinic.

Sarah narrowed her eyes, weak yet enraged.

Howard leapt behind the breakfast bar and pulled out his Ruger. Sarah leapt up from behind the breakfast table and zeroed in on Ashley. Time for a little payback.

Paul barrelled into Sarah from the side, knocking her aim off so she fired a round into the ceiling. He followed it up by almost breaking her jaw with a punch. She sprawled onto the ground and couldn't get up. All of her injuries coalesced and left her a sagging mess on the floor.

Paul stomped over to her and raised his foot above her head. He was about to stamp on her skull when Howard let off a shot. It missed, but it was enough to send Paul running to join his daughter at the back of the kitchen. Howard tried to get off a follow-up shot, but Ashley fired at him first, forcing him behind the breakfast bar.

Sarah was still trying to catch her breath when the Fosters escaped through a back door.

Howard knelt next to Sarah. "You saved my hide. How did you know she had a gun hidden in the fruit bowl?"

Sarah blinked away the stars in her vision. "Fruit and I have a long history. Now come on, let's get after them."

As if in reply, gunfire rang outside, preceding the sound of an engine starting up.

Sarah flinched. "Mandy!"

Howard took off, and Sarah staggered after him. She held her gun in front of her, ready to take down anyone who even looked at her wrong.

Howard yanked open the front door and ducked out onto the driveway. The sleek black Audi had rocketed, shunting the MCU's Jaguar out of the way and heading down the road. Lights in the nearby houses flipped on like beacons, alerted by the gunfire, and stock car racing.

"We really need to get a mechanic on staff," Howard said, shaking his head.

Sarah looked at the crumpled wing of the Jaguar and clucked. "Too bad we don't have the budget for it."

"Oh so it's 'we' now, is it?"

"Come on." She raced over to the Jaguar and found Mandy still sitting in the driver's seat. It was clear from the shattered front windows that Ashley and her father had fired at him as they made their escape. He looked none too happy. Sarah slid in beside the big man, and Howard threw himself across the back seat.

Mandy slammed his foot on the accelerator.

The Foster's Audi was fast—it roared through the neighbourhood like an angry bear—but Mandy's Jaguar was quick too, deceptively so for such a big car. It wasn't long before they gained a few yards on the Audi.

"Their car's quick," Sarah said, clocking their own speedometer at seventy.

"It's a TT," Howard said from the back seat. "They have a few horsepower on us, but we have Mandy."

To prove the point, the TT screeched around a corner, while Mandy seemed to float around it. The Audi raced for the highway, and they followed, just two car distances behind.

But that distance soon became larger.

"They're getting away!" Sarah shouted.

Howard grunted. "We can't keep up with them on the straight, but we can cut them off at the exit." He pulled out his mob-sat and put another call through to Mattock. "We're in pursuit of target, heading north on the A4114, Abingdon Road. Requesting backup at River Thames, south side." Howard listened for a second and then put the mob-sat back in his pocket. He leant forward between the front seats. "Mattock will be at the river in six minutes."

Sarah hissed. "That's going to be too late. We will be at the river any minute."

Howard went blank, searching for an idea. Up ahead, the TT continued gaining distance. Sarah pulled out her gun and took aim through the side window, firing a shot. The discharge made no sound in the rushing wind, and the bullet seemed to disappear. She fired several more times, but there was too much distance between the two cars. "Shit," she muttered. "They're going to get away."

"No, they're not," Howard said. He turned around and rifled through the back compartment behind the seats. What he came up with both shocked and delighted Sarah.

"Now you're turning me on," she said.

Howard held the L129A1 Sharpshooter against his shoulder and grinned. "A gift from our American cousins. I guess size matters."

The morning roads were empty, and the Fosters were gaining distance every second. "You need to hurry," she said. "They will be out of range soon."

Howard rolled down his window and shoved his upper body out of the car, righting the rifle against his shoulder. A few seconds passed and then he let off an ear-piercing shot.

Sarah flinched.

The TT continued speeding away.

Howard fired again. This time the TT jerked left. For a second, it looked like it would flip, but its safety systems kicked in, and the tyres regained their grip on the road.

A thick strip of rubber flew from the TT and whizzed by the Jaguar's windscreen. Sarah smiled as she realized that Howard had hit the rear tyre. Despite the damage, the TT still sped along.

"They must have run flats," Sarah realised.

"Doesn't matter," Howard said. "It'll slow them down."

Mandy leant forward behind the wheel, his eyes narrowing and his shoulders stiffening. It wouldn't be long before he caught them up to the TT.

Sarah waited. Should she fire at the TT, or would Mandy try to run it off the road safely? She'd already killed Leanne Foster tonight. Could she take more lives? Did she even care? The Fosters had given up their right to mercy when they'd gotten involved with Hesbani. There was no obvious link yet, but Sarah knew that *Shab Bekhier* was behind this. A shiver ran down her neck.

They were right behind the TT now. Sarah checked her watch: 5:12AM.

"Get ready," Howard said. He'd placed the Sharpshooter down and was holding his pistol now. "Mandy, try to run them off the road as soon as it's safe. If they refuse to stop, Sarah and I will have to take them out."

Mandy brought the Jaguar up on the TT's rear bumper. The Audi's rear tyre had gone flat now, and the vehicle hitched from side to side as Paul fought against the steering. Sarah could see Ashley sitting beside him, looking back at them. Sarah gave the girl the middle finger.

Ashley fired back at them.

Sarah ducked as the Jaguar's windscreen shattered, but she was right back up and returning fire. The TT veered back and forth, still keeping its speed above fifty.

Sarah let off another shot just as a ricochet bounced of the Jaguar's roof and almost took the other side of her face. Her ears were ringing, and in the distance, she could hear the sirens of alerted police. She wondered what would happen if they apprehended her. The MCU was supposed to be secret, so what would the police have to say about the dead woman she'd just left in a middle-class neighbourhood? How much influence did MCU have?

Ashley let off another barrage and forced Sarah to duck back down in her seat.

"River's coming up," Howard informed them. "Let's hope Mattock is there waiting for us."

Mandy yanked the steering wheel and brought the Jaguar up around the side of the slowing TT. As Sarah looked to her left, she saw Paul gripping the steering wheel and facing forward defiantly.

Ashley leant over her father's lap and let off another shot.

Mandy trod on the brake, dropping speed and pulling Sarah out of harm's way before Ashley had opportunity to place her aim. Sarah turned to thank him, but cried out when she saw him bleeding and half-conscious behind the wheel. His black clothing made the source of the blood hard to detect, but the splatter around his neck and face made it clear he'd been hit.

Oh shit!

Mandy slumped against the steering wheel and the Jaguar went sideways. Sarah and Howard were powerless to do anything as the vehicle hopped the pavement and smashed headfirst into a transit van parked at the side of the road.

Sarah's body turned to jelly and her bones rattled inside her skin. Her head bucked so hard that she thought it would fall off her shoulders. Then, suddenly, she could see only white.

Her eyes remained closed for a while, as she came to terms with the fact she was still alive, but slowly she opened them.

Something smothered her face, making her panic. It took several anguished seconds before she realised it was the airbag. She pawed and swatted at it until it deflated and got out of her way. When it did, she could see nothing but pavement

Mandy hung upside down from the driver's seat, held in place by his seatbelt. He wasn't moving and blood dripped down his forehead, pattering against the roof beneath him. Howard was lost some place in the back.

The only way Sarah could go was ahead, so she dragged herself. She shuffled forward, kicking with her legs and pulling with her fingertips. Blood leaked from a gash on the back of her hand, and she moaned. She couldn't lose any more blood—already felt close to passing out. Pulling herself into a shaft of sunlight, she crawled into the hole left by the missing windscreen. It was a tight fit, but she made her way through. What made it more unsettling was that she'd done this before. This time, instead of the heated sands of Afghanistan, Sarah pulled herself out onto the coarse pavements of England.

The sound of footsteps and Paul Foster was pointing a gun

in Sarah's face. Ashley stood beside her father, sneering. "Just kill the bitch, dad."

"I will, but you get out of here first."

"No way."

Paul looked at his daughter. "Don't you hear that? The police will be here any minute. Get out of here now while I deal with this. I'll be with you soon. You know where to go. There's still work to be done."

Ashley took off like lightning. The girl had nine-lives. Sarah didn't have the energy left to take them all. She was done, defeated.

"I'm sorry about this," Paul told her, still pointing the gun. "But you're part of the problem."

"What problem?" Sarah was genuinely curious. She didn't want to die in ignorance.

"The problem of being a human being in today's world. You're fighting to protect a system that's all wrong. We live by greed and selfishness. We take what we want and leave our victims to suffer. Being rich is the goal everyone strives for, so that the poor can clean their toilets and eat the cheap food they don't want. We live in a world where 99% of us suffer and toil to make life wonderful for the other 1%. Don't you think that's wrong?"

Sarah nodded. It sounded so reasonable.

"Again, I'm really sorry about this." Paul pressed the gun barrel against her forehead.

No! This would not happen again. Sarah had been on her knees waiting for death twenty-four hours ago, thanks to the Foster family, and she was sick of it. She'd lived through the clinic car park shootout, and she would live now. She was done being a victim.

Sarah sprung to her feet and barreled into Paul just as he was going to pull the trigger. The sudden blow caught him off guard, and he went staggering backwards. Sarah struck him square in the chest with the heel of her palm. The air went rushing out of him, and his face puffed up like a balloon. She went to strike again with an elbow to the temple, but Paul recovered and punched her in the gut, then rugby tackled her as she was reeling backwards.

As soon as Sarah hit her back, Paul head butted her in the face. She tried to shake the blow off, but as soon as she did, there was a gun pointed in her face again.

"You just made this a whole lot easier," Paul said, snarling.

He pulled the trigger.

14

WEAKNESS

AFGHANISTAN, 2008

Sarah didn't know how long she'd been asleep when they dragged her from the cell. They took Hamish too, who'd recovered enough from his beating to share his bread and water with Sarah. The soldier killed by the IED had been one of the privates, not Sarah's corporal as she'd thought. Hamish had been dragged out of the Snatch after Sarah was taken. He'd tried to put up a fight, but had been beaten bloody for it.

Now, they were being manhandled and dragged out of their cell. Every time Sarah stumbled, she received an elbow in the back or a sandal up her backside. She was subdued, but Hamish was irate. He bellowed and cursed, even when the men slapped and punched him for his defiance.

"Shut up, Hamish. They will kill you if you don't shut up."

Hamish huffed. "They're gunna kill us both anyhow. Why make it easy for 'em? I'm Glaswegian. They can break my bones, but not my spirit."

"They're going to let us go," Sarah told him. "Al Sharir told me so last night."

Hamish looked at her. "Really?"

"Yes, so behave."

Hamish caught another shove in his back, but this time he remained quiet. They were taken to a dusty yard, walled off on all sides. There was a group of men there, Al-Sharir and Wazir Hesbani among them. A boy knelt, crying. He looked around fifteen, wearing jeans and a t-shirt. It was his fuzzy beard and cheap sandals that gave him away as a native Afghan.

Al-Sharir summoned Sarah and Hamish and had them lowered to their knees beside the boy. Sarah gritted her teeth at the pain in her wounded thigh. The hole had been weeping blood all night.

Al-Sharir gave her a thin smile. "Hello, Captain, how are you feeling today?"

Sarah looked him in the eye. "Looking forward to you keeping your word."

"I will keep my word, do not worry."

Sarah let out a breath. She'd been anxious that Al-Sharir would change his mind. It was a relief to hear that he hadn't. "Thank you," she said.

"We have business to attend to first," Hesbani said. "We won't keep you longer than we have to."

Sarah frowned. What business was there? She wanted to go back to Camp Bastion.

A large crowd assembled in a semi-circle around them. Hesbani pointed at the teenaged boy. "This man has been found guilty of murder. Under Islamic law, he is to be put to death."

The boy wept.

"He's just a child," Sarah said in disgust.

"He has been found guilty of the worst crime. He has slaughtered and must be held accountable to Allah."

Hesbani struck the boy, bloodying his mouth. A man

standing in the crowd caught the boy and kept him upright on his knees. The boy cried out louder.

"Leave him be, yer tosser," Hamish spat.

Hesbani glanced at Hamish. "What is *tosser*?"

"It's a fella what hits kids."

Hesbani sneered. "Then I am, indeed, a *tosser*." He struck the boy again.

Sarah closed her eyes. "Please stop."

Al-Sharir raised a hand to stop Hesbani. He took a step towards Sarah. "Would you like to know this boy's crimes? His actions have caused many deaths."

Sarah knew what the kid would be guilty of, it was clear from his clothing. "He's been helping the allied forces, informing on the Taliban." The boy had probably grown up in a village controlled by NATO forces, lived on their handouts, and begged for Western clothing. "He's just a kid doing what he thinks is *right*. Leave him alone."

Al-Sharir stared at her. "He is Taliban."

Sarah's jaw dropped. "No..."

Hesbani sniggered. "Confused by his clothing, are you, Captain? He dress that way to get close to Western troops. He spy on them from only feet away. IED that take you and your men was his creation. A clever boy, no?"

Sarah frowned. "That doesn't make any sense. The IED belongs to you."

Al-Sharir shook his head. "Taliban leave IED. I just clean up mess. That is not why boy is here. He has been setting up bomb for fun. He is evil."

Sarah looked at the sobbing child and struggled with it. "I don't believe you."

Hesbani laughed. "Why? Because he is just boy? He is killer. You are looking at a Taliban, trained from birth to make and set bombs to kill your soldiers. He has killed many dozens. Your own men among them. Murder is all he knows."

"It is true," Al-Sharir said. "He is well known to us. He has a talent for death. The Taliban have trained many innocent children to be killers. Once they reach a certain age, they are irredeemable."

"But… what do you care what he does against the West?"

"I care because every death he cause bring more in return. I believe in fighting for Afghanistan freedom, but buried bomb and booby trap not way to get it. No honour in creating something that kill children as easy as soldier. Last week, one of boy's bombs kill innocent girl, five year old. Her father saw her blow up. He bring remains back to village and weep for days. I see it with my own eyes."

Sarah swallowed. Part of her had stopped caring what had happened to the boy, but another part reminded her it was not the boy's fault; he'd been raised by the Taliban. "Hand the boy over to Camp Bastion. Why cause more death? You said you want the fighting to stop, so cooperate."

"Cooperate with foreign invaders?" Hesbani snarled. "We deal with own problems, enforce own laws. We want death to end, but can only happen if we unite against West."

"My friend is right," said Al-Sharir. "Why should we hand boy over when it is our laws he has broken? You wish imprison boy when Allah demand deeper punishment."

"Kill the bastard." Hamish shrugged. "If you don't, our lot will once they get him."

Sarah stared at her corporal. "What?"

"We lost three young lads to that IED. The kid deserves an execution. He's Taliban."

"That's not who we are," Sarah said. "We're here to help this country, not execute its children. We are not executioners."

"No," Hesbani said, "That is what we are. The boy has been found guilty by Islamic law."

Al-Sharir raised his hand to Hesbani. "Perhaps Captain is right. Maybe we compromise. Boy does not have to die." Al-Sharir placed a hand against the boy's bruised cheek and said, "*Ta shaista starge lare.*" Then he gave Hesbani a nod, and the boy was dragged to his feet by the man.

"Your lucky day," Hesbani said, grabbing the boy by his throat and holding him up. With his free hand he slid a rusty *peshkabz* from a scabbard on his belt. The ceremonial dagger was commonplace amongst the hill tribes of Afghanistan, but not so common in the South.

The boy yelled in terror, kicking his legs so hard that both sandals flew off his feet. Hesbani controlled the boy with a single hand while waving the dagger in front of the boy's face with the other.

Hesbani shoved the dagger into the boy's left eye.

Then the right.

The boy slumped to the ground, howling in a way that wasn't human. He clutched his ruined eyes and convulsed in the dirt.

Sarah lurched forward and threw up.

Hamish moaned beside her.

"Your turn now," Hesbani said, grabbing Hamish by the back of his shirt and tugging him to his feet.

Hamish struggled and was struck across his face. Tears blinded him, and the fight left him.

Sarah cried out to Al-Sharir. "Leave him alone. You said you would let us go."

"I said that I would let *you* go."

"Please. Please, don't kill him."

Al-Sharir tapped his chin with his forefinger and seemed to think for a few seconds. Eventually, he nodded and said,

"Okay. I have idea. Wazir, take his eyes. We send back with captain as gift to British camp."

"No!" Sarah screamed.

"Just kill me," Hamish moaned. "I'd rather die."

Sarah tried to get up, but a firm set of hands from the crowd held her down. Hesbani kicked Hamish in the back of the legs, sending him to his knees.

Al-Sharir stood in front of Sarah. "Do not struggle, Captain. You have innocent one inside you, remember? It is the only reason you yet live."

Hamish looked at her with wide eyes, surprised by the revelation.

"Just let us go," she begged. "You'll just make things worse if you execute a British soldier."

Al-Sharir raised an eyebrow. "Ah, but I save more than I kill. Boy killer will set no more bombs. Any debt I have to British Army are even, no? I tell you what, I let you decide corporal's fate. I already been fair to you, but still you ask more. So, do I have Wazir kill corporal, or should he take eyes?"

"Neither. Please, neither."

Al-Sharir nodded. "Okay, third choice: I let him go and blind *you* instead. Your child safe and corporal will live. Your face already very bad, no? At least you not have to look in mirror."

"Y-you're sick!"

"You offend me. I am being more than kind. Make choice now."

Sarah caught Hamish's gaze, and they looked at each other in complete horror. Neither of them made a sound.

"Make decision!" Al-Sharir shouted at her.

"I can't!"

Al-Sharir's face grew thunderous. "Fine. Choices now

shrunk. I blind you or kill him. Your sight or his life."

Sarah couldn't find her voice.

Al-Sharir folded his arms. "Fine. Wazir, take Captain's eyes. We send corporal back unharmed, to tell everybody what hero is his commander."

"No!" Sarah gushed in floods of tears. "K-kill him. Don't hurt me. Kill him."

Hamish stared at Sarah with bloodshot, terror-filled eyes. He looked truly stunned.

Sarah stared at the dirt.

Al-Sharir huffed. "And there we have it. You British have forever seen yourselves noble and just, yet none of you prepared to suffer for convictions. You rather watch friend die than lose something of your own. Your greed, your selfishness will be downfall. Wazir, get over with. I sick of being around these soulless devils."

Sarah couldn't help but watch. She'd sentenced her corporal to death; the least she could do was watch what her decision had wrought.

Hesbani took the blood-soaked dagger and swiped it across Hamish's throat. Blood spewed onto the sand, and Hamish fell backwards, clutching his opened neck in silent terror. Sarah looked away and wept as the crowd of cheering men yanked her to her feet and dragged her away.

OXFORD, 2014

Paul Foster was dead before he pulled the trigger. His head exploded in a cloud of mist, and he slumped, face down, on top of Sarah. Sarah just lay there. She had been about to die, but she was still alive. Somebody had saved her life, but who?

Paul's dead body was dragged aside. Sarah's rescuer, a middle-aged man with a face made of rock stared down at her.

A large scar sliced upward from his forehead and cut a furrow along the top of his shaved head like the seam on a tennis ball.

"You all right, luv?"

Sarah couldn't respond.

The man patted her with harsh, all-business hands. His expression was oddly compassionate, considering the harshness of his battle-hardened face. "Are you in pain?" he asked her.

Sarah shook her head.

"Can you stand?"

Sarah nodded.

"Let's give it a go, then."

Sarah took his hand, and he yanked her to her feet. She dusted herself off and tried to regain her senses. She went to speak, but her rescuer bolted off toward the crumpled mess that had once been a Jaguar XFR.

There were other men around too, perhaps six in total. They all wore urban combat suits covered in pouches. In the middle of the road was the Foster's Audi TT. Its flat tyre had brought it to a stop.

Sarah watched the chaos for a moment, but then snapped back into reality. "Howard!" she yelped. "Mandy!"

Both men were still inside the wrecked Jaguar. She had to get them out of there. She raced to the upturned Jaguar. The response team was already forcing the wrecked vehicle's frame apart with the Jaws of Life.

"Stay back, Captain. We have this under control," said the man who rescued her.

"You're Mattock," she said, turning back.

"Yes, I am, and you're Captain Stone. What the bleedin' hell happened here, luv?"

"I don't know." It was the truth. Sarah's mind was a blur. "We were trying to run them off the road. Mandy got shot."

Mattock grimaced. "Mandy took a bullet?"

Sarah swallowed. She'd never exchanged two words with the giant from MCU, but she hated knowing he was hurt. "I don't know how bad it was," was all she could say.

"How about Howard? Is he okay?"

"I don't know. He was in the back."

"We'll 'ave 'em out soon enough, luv, but we need to get you out of here. The Old Bill are coming."

To prove his point, a fleet of police cars skidded to a stop in the middle of the road.

"What will you tell them?" Sarah asked Mattock.

"It'll be messy, but I can get this squared away, but with Mandy and Howard incapacitated, we can't afford to have you retained for questioning. We need to get you out of here and back to the Earthworm, sharpish."

"I'm not leaving Howard and Mandy."

"I'm not giving you a choice, Captain. You look like shit, and you're the only witness to this entire fuck fest. If the Old Bill get 'old of yer, they'll be questioning you till the Queen farts. All the while, there are bad guys out there plotting their next move."

Sarah nodded. She couldn't afford to be retained into custody. Even if she wanted to stay, Mattock looked like he could crush her until she changed her mind. "Okay," she said. "What should I do?"

"Take this." Mattock handed her a slim, electronic device. "It's an MCU mob-sat. Take off now, find someplace safe, and then call Director Palu. He'll have you extracted. Don't let the plods catch you until I have this all squared away."

The police were getting out of their cars and heading toward the scene. Sarah wanted to run, but she couldn't take her eyes off the upturned Jaguar. Howard and Mandy were still inside, and it felt wrong to leave them. She'd made a habit of leaving people behind, and she cursed herself for it. But what could she do?

I can catch the sons of bitches responsible, that's what.

"Move your arse," Mattock shouted.

Sarah bolted, disappearing into an alleyway. It was the same direction that Ashley Foster had gone. Maybe if she was lucky, they would run into one another.

15

STRENGTH

It was 7:30AM when Sarah stopped running. She reached a bus stop and keeled over, collapsing on the bench and dangling her head between her legs. She could lie low there for a while, pretending she was waiting for a bus. Hiding in plain sight.

She pulled the mob-sat from Dr Bennett's blazer and switched it on. She hit the icon marked, CONTACTS, and a long list of names appeared, including Prime Minister Breslow herself.

A bus stopped at the side of the road. Sarah remained seated until it closed its doors and drove away. When it did, she searched the contacts list and found DIRECTOR PALU.

Palu picked up, but said nothing, so Sarah stated her name.

"Sarah, are you all right? Mattock just reported in; he said you had to clear the area."

"I'm fine. I'm a mess, but that was true when you hired me. I need picking up."

"Where are you?"

Sarah looked around. She spotted a bus timetable and

read out the address. "I'm sitting in a bus shelter in Botley. Bus stop 12, Raleigh Park Road."

"Lie low. Bradley's on his way."

"Roger that."

"Are you injured?"

"Only emotionally." Sarah cleared her throat. It'd been a joke, but it was kind of true. "I... killed Leanne Foster. Mattock killed Paul Foster, and Ashley got away. The whole family is involved in this somehow."

Palu exhaled. "Dr Bennett and I are looking into every lead we have. We'll figure this out. Just sit tight, okay?"

"Will do. I'll report in if I have to move."

"Roger that."

Sarah slunk forwards on the bench and watched the morning traffic. She wondered if anybody else would die today. If Hesbani struck again, anarchy would reign. The people of Great Britain were a tough bunch, but they were unused to being victims. They were fighters, not defenders.

Forty minutes later, Bradley skidded up in front of the bus stop, driving the remaining Jaguar from MCU. As soon as Sarah closed the car door behind her, she felt safe again. She was glad to see Bradley, and he looked glad to see her.

"Are you okay, Captain?"

Sarah sighed. "I'm not a captain, so stop calling me that. Just get me back to the Earthworm."

Bradley said nothing, but he looked at her from the corner of his eye, then said, "Howard's okay."

Sarah stared at him. "Really?"

Bradley nodded. "He has a broken arm, but otherwise he's okay."

"What about Mandy?"

Bradley went quiet.

"Bradley!"

"We don't know yet. He took a slug in his lung. Mattock took him to John Radcliffe Hospital. He'll tell us as soon as he knows anything."

Sarah let her head drop. She was glad about Howard, but Mandy had taken a bullet meant for her. "What do we have on Ashley Foster?" she asked. "You can't let her get away with this."

"*We* can't," said Bradley. "Bennett and Palu are finding everything they can. There has to be a reason the Fosters are involved in whatever's going on. We'll find a way to link them to Hesbani, and then it's just a matter of time."

Sarah rubbed at her scars and thought. Paul Foster had been concerned about his daughter getting to safety, the same way any father would be. Something must have happened to make a middle-class family man so militant. Finding out Paul Foster's trigger could be the key to figuring everything out.

Sarah would say her goodbyes and get out of this situation before she got any deeper. "Is Howard back at the Earthworm?" she asked.

"One of Mattock's men took him back," Bradley confirmed. "I heard he reached you in the nick of time."

Sarah pictured Paul Foster kneeling over her, intending to pull the trigger. "Saved my life. Just like you did back at the clinic."

Bradley blushed. "Least I got a shot off. I'm improving."

Sarah didn't allow him to make light of the matter. "You need to do better. You could have ended the situation sooner. We would have Dr Cartwright in our custody if you'd taken Ashley down. Everything that's happened this morning is because you didn't pull the trigger the second you were supposed to." Sarah remembered how quickly she'd pulled the trigger on Leanne. She hadn't hesitated. "Soon as you're sure, you need to act. People die if you don't."

Bradley looked like he was about to erupt into tears.

Sarah softened. "Look, I'm not one to give you a lecture. Since Howard brought me in, I've been nothing but a liability. But unlike me, you're sticking around. You need to get better at this."

Bradley nodded and seemed determined. "I will."

"So you're not going to quit anymore?"

"Not while there are people like Hesbani in the world. I want to do this. I'll get better, I promise."

"Don't promise me. Promise yourself, because if you don't get better, you'll be dead, and you're too young and sweet for that to be okay."

Bradley chuckled. "Thank you, Captain."

"It's Sarah."

"Sorry. Thank you, Sarah."

Sarah cleared her throat. "Now, get me back to Dr Bennet so she can give me more of the good stuff. My head has cleared, but the fuzziness left a shitload of hurt in its place."

Bradley pulled onto the highway and picked up speed. "So, what are you doing all the way over in Botley?"

Sarah shrugged. "I had to run. I headed in the same direction Ashley did, kept on going, but never found her. Eventually my legs gave up, and when I stopped I was in Botley."

"It's a nice little village," Bradley said, glancing out his window. "The kind of place where they still keep budgies as pets."

Sarah frowned as something occurred to her. "Knutsford was a nice little village, too."

Bradley's expression turned sour. "So were Studley, Arborfield, and Dartmouth."

Sarah didn't enjoy the feeling in her gut, like toxic spores erupting. "You don't think Botley could be a target, do you?"

"I don't know. It's a long shot. Ashley could have gone

anywhere. All you know is the direction she started in. Even if she *was* in Botley, it doesn't mean the village is a target."

"Get Palu on the radio."

Bradley obliged and thumbed a button on the steering wheel. The audible sound of dialing took over the car, and then silence as Palu answered.

"Palu, it's Sarah."

"Sarah. Are you with Bradley?"

"Yes, we're together. We think we might have a lead on *Shab Bekhier*'s next target. The village of Botley, on the outskirts of Oxford."

Silence.

Bradley glanced at Sarah, then tapped the dashboard with his finger. "Sir?"

Palu came back. "Dr Bennett has found something, a reason the Fosters might have a grudge."

"Go on," Sarah said.

"The HS2 link."

Sarah and Bradley exchanged confused looks. Sarah said, "The train line the Government is building? What the hell does that have to do with anything?"

"Paul Foster and his family were forced to sell their home to make way for the proposed route. Paul built the home himself twenty-five years ago and raised his family there for two decades. He had a son who died of Leukaemia last year and was buried on the property."

"That's weird," said Bradley.

"But not illegal. When the Government forced the sale of the land, they also relocated the boy's body."

"Kicked them out of their own home," said Bradley, tutting.

"They were compensated, of course," Palu added, "but that might be why the family has a grudge against the country."

There was a short pause before Palu said, "There's also another link. Paul Foster runs a construction company, and part of his services include demolition. We believe he may have been the one supplying the explosives for the attacks, maybe even designed the suicide vests. He has a license to obtain high explosives."

Sarah punched the dashboard. "All *this* because he was forced to sell his mansion? There has to be more to it than that."

"Perhaps," said Palu, "but we're still working on it."

"What does this have to do with Botley?" Bradley asked.

"Paul Fosters's construction company is based there."

Sarah's eyes narrowed. "What's the address?" Palu gave it to them. "You need to send Mattock there right now."

"Negative. Mattock is taking care of Agent Dobbs. You and Bradley are our only available assets."

Sarah swallowed. "Palu, I'm not the right woman for this job. I can barely stand up and every time something happens, I end up on my knees with a gun in my face."

"You don't have a choice. You're all we have."

Sarah said nothing. For the first time since she lost Thomas and their baby, she felt fear. Hesbani had been the man responsible for destroying her entire life. Did she have it in her to face him if it came to it? She couldn't even close her eyes at night without seeing his snarling face and whimpering.

"We're on it," Bradley said. "Re-brief when we arrive at destination."

"Roger that," Palu said.

The line went dead.

Sarah felt her heart pound in her chest. Her body was agony. The only place that didn't hurt was her face; for once, her scars were numb.

Bradley started back towards Botley. He noticed Sarah staring out the window. "Hey, come back to me."

"I'm here," she said.

"We can deal with this," he told her. "Ashley Foster is alone and desperate. We can take her in, but I need you with me." When Sarah hesitated, Bradley said, "You're the one always telling me not to freeze up, so now I need you to follow your own advice and man up."

Sarah glared at him. "Man up? Does it look like I have a dick?"

Bradley shrugged. "Sometimes it does. You're kind of intimidating."

"Intimidating?"

"Yeah, I don't know if you know, but you're kind of snarly. You remind me of an abused Jack Russell Terrier my nan adopted. It bit anyone who tried to pet it. The only reason it was like that, though, was because it was mistreated and abandoned. It loved my nan though, and as soon as it realised it could trust her, it became the most loyal pet in the world. That's kind of like you, Captain. You've had some bad experiences, but I know that there's a good, loyal person underneath all that snarling. I just want you to know that you can trust me."

Sarah bristled, softened, then bristled again. "I can only trust you if you pull the trigger when you're supposed to."

"I promise to pull the trigger when it's needed, but only if you get your head back in the game."

The past was pulling Sarah down, dragging her into a vacuous pit of despair, but there was a chance hanging in front of her—a chance to change things. She couldn't live with the anger inside her anymore; she had to let it out, needed to take back her life and her self-respect. Afghanistan had taken more than just her face, it had taken part of her soul, too. Perhaps there was still time to get that back.

"Okay, Bradley," she said. "Step on it. We're not going to let that psychopath get away again. This time, she's mine."

Fifteen minutes later, they were back in Botley. They entered onto a high street, passing by a Roman-style Market Hall nestled between Tudor houses and other mid-century buildings. They found Foster Homes & Construction at the far end of the village centre, hidden down a side-street beside a small builder's yard. The lights were off, but there were men at work in the adjacent business.

Bradley parked the Jaguar up on the curb. "You ready?"

Sarah breathed. She felt like shit. "I'm ready."

They headed to the unlit offices of Foster's construction company. Sarah crept up to the window and peered inside. There was nothing except the flashing LED of an answering phone.

Bradley gave the front entrance a shove, and they were both surprised when it opened. Both of them took out their guns, clicking the safeties off.

Bradley slid inside first, Sarah close behind. Instinctively, they moved to opposite sides of the room. Sarah's old training came back to her like it had been yesterday.

"I don't think anyone's here," whispered Bradley. "We must've missed her."

Sarah didn't respond. Her focus was on the answering machine. It was blinking. She stepped over to the machine and pressed 'PLAY.'

Bradley lowered his weapon and came to listen. They were both disappointed when they heard an automated message for PPI insurance claims. Sarah used the barrel of her SIG to press another button on the machine.

"What are you doing?" Bradley asked her.

"Checking the saved messages."

Another voicemail played. Sarah knew the voice well from the previous two tapes she'd viewed at MCU—and from her nightmares.

"*Two Syrian freedom fighters killed by British Peacekeepers. Balance the scales.*"

"That was Hesbani," Sarah said.

Bradley frowned. "What does it mean?"

"I don't know. Come on, we need to comb this place, see if we can—"

A noise caught their attention. Bradley and Sarah drew their guns towards the back of the room.

Ashley Foster was standing in the doorway of one of the offices, looking surprised. She didn't draw a weapon, which let Sarah know that she no longer had a gun.

"Don't fucking move," Sarah growled. "I'm just dying to take your head off."

Ashley snickered. "With that poxy thing? I'd be surprised if the bullet even reaches me."

Sarah pointed the gun at Ashley's face. "Let's test that theory."

Some of the defiance left Ashley's eyes, and she looked like an unsure teenager for the first time. Bradley took a step towards her while Sarah kept her talking. "What's this all about, Ashley? Your mum and dad are both dead. For what?"

The news of her father's death struck Ashley, and she recoiled. Sarah wondered what it was like to care so much for a parent that it physically hurt to hear they were dead. When she one day got the news that her own father was dead, Sarah imagined feeling only relief.

There were tears in Ashley's eyes, but a growl on her lips. "I'll kill you."

"Not if I kill you first."

"Give it up, Ashley," Bradley said. "Nobody else has to get hurt. Just let us take you in, and we can hear your story. We'll listen."

"Yeah," said Sarah, deciding to try the soft approach. "You look like shit, Ashley. Let us take care of you." It was true. The girl was pale, sweating, and looked in pain.

Ashley wavered. She could bolt, but seemed to gravitate towards Bradley, ready to give herself up. She looked like a screwed-up teenager in over her head. Bradley obviously recognised that and was keeping her calm by playing the caring stranger. Sarah was ready to pull the trigger the moment it didn't look like it was working.

Bradley took another step towards Ashley, holding his hand out to her. "Let us help you."

Ashley held up her bandaged hand. Blood leaked down her wrist from where Bradley had shot her. "You've already helped enough."

Bradley lowered his gun, pointing it at the floor, and took another step forward. "You gave me no choice. Don't force me to do it again. Nobody has to get hurt."

Sarah kept her own gun trained on Ashley. "Bradley, stay where you are. Ashley, put your hands behind your head and get down on your knees."

Ashley's lower lip quivered. "Please. I just want to see my dad."

"It's okay," said Bradley. "It's over now."

"Bradley, step back." Sarah didn't like how close he was getting to Ashley.

Ashley broke down in tears. She turned away and hugged herself, shaking as she wept. Bradley kept on moving towards her, his hand out in front of him, his gun pointed at the floor.

Sarah raised her voice. "For fuck sake, Bradley, keep away

from her! Ashley, get on your knees now, before I blow your goddamn brains all over the wall."

Ashley spun around, a flash of metal gliding through the air towards Bradley's throat.

Sarah cried out, unable to let a shot off as the risk of hitting her partner was too high. The bitch would slice his throat.

Bradley ducked under the blade narrowly avoiding it. Crouching, he threw a left hook at Ashley's ribcage and sent her stumbling backwards. Then he pulled the trigger.

The dark room flashed white as the gunshot echoed off the walls. Ashley screamed, hopping on one leg as blood gushed out of her mangled foot.

Sarah closed the distance between them and was just in time to catch Ashley in her arms. The girl stared at her, a mixture of agony and rage on her face. "The bastard shot me in the foot."

Sarah smiled. "Lucky you. I'd have shot you in the face." She head butted Ashley, who flopped to the floor unconscious. Then Sarah grinned at Bradley. "God," she said to him, "I've been dying to do that."

16

RUIN

Getting Ashley back to MCU had been an ordeal. She woke up from the headbutt not five minutes later, screaming because of the pain in her foot. Sarah was already weak, without having to wrestle an adrenaline-fueled girl, ten years younger than her. Bradley had done most of the lifting, but seemed guilty about shooting Ashley. Sarah made sure he knew he had done the right thing. Bradley could have killed her, and it would have been the right thing.

The worst part of trying to get Ashley to their car was the workers next door. They obviously heard the gunshot, and the whole lot of them came looking. When they saw Ashley bleeding and being dragged into the back of a Jaguar, they raised all kinds of hell. When they threatened to call the police, Sarah remembered Mattock's warning not to get apprehended. She pulled out her gun and fired a shot into the air. The men ran off.

Bradley took the wheel while Sarah tried to restrain Ashley in the back. When the girl became too much of a handful, Sarah smashed the butt of her SIG against her temple, knocking her out again. The rest of the drive was blessedly peaceful.

Palu met them at the abandoned farm, ready with handcuffs. When Ashley finally came to again, she was sullen and silent. Sarah assumed this was because of the headbutt, but when they led Ashley from the car to the Earthworm's concealed entrance, she keeled over and vomited. The girl looked unwell. Sarah wondered if she'd given Ashley a concussion.

They carried Ashley into the Earthworm, heading for Dr Bennett's infirmary.

"Once she's been treated, she'll be taken to the holding cells in the middle section of the Earthworm," Bradley explained en route.

They reached the infirmary and waited while Dr Bennett worked inside. A little over an hour later, she came out to talk to them.

"Are you done, doctor? I need to talk to her," Sarah said, tapping her foot.

Bennett sniffed. "The girl's a mess—wounds all over. I'm not sure how much she'll be able to give you. Why don't you let her rest for a while?"

Sarah couldn't believe what she was hearing. "You do know that Ashley Foster and her family might be responsible for four suicide attacks?"

"She's just a girl. We don't know what she's guilty of yet."

Sarah hissed. "She shot me. You should know, you patched me up."

"If you need to talk to her, fine, but I think we should let Director Palu decide. He's the one in charge here, not you."

"Let her in," Palu ordered, appearing from one of the adjacent hallways and walking towards them.

Dr Bennett folded her arms. "Very well. I have the patient on painkillers, so she's a little drowsy. Go easy on her."

"The girl is a psychopath," Sarah said. "She tried to slice Bradley's throat."

"Until I pulled the trigger," Bradley commented.

Sarah smiled back. "Yeah, that's a hand and a foot you have on your resume now."

Dr Bennett opened the door to the infirmary and let them through. Ashley scowled at them like a foul smell had descended upon her.

Sarah was surprised to see that Howard was there, too, with his left arm in a cast. "You look like you've been in a car accident," Sarah said.

Howard smirked. "I should have been strapped in." His expression sombred. "Any of you heard about Mandy?"

Sarah shook her head.

"Mandy was in surgery the last time I spoke with Mattock," Palu told them.

Everybody was silent for a moment.

Ashley grabbed their attention. "Big fucking deal. My parents are *dead* because of you lot. I'm glad your man is suffering; I'm just sorry I didn't kill him. Where the hell am I anyway? You people aren't police. The guy I shot is probably dead by now, so why don't you hurry up and charge me, because you're not getting anything out of me."

Sarah clenched her fists. Mandy had taken a bullet meant for her. "Keep talking and you'll wish you were dead."

Ashley laughed. Despite her petulance, she looked sick. Her breathing was irregular, and her skin was moist and translucent.

"Is she going to be okay?" Bradley asked, referring to Ashley. "She looks bad."

Dr Bennett shrugged. "She should be fine. She's missing

two toes and her hand is infected, but her injuries aren't life-threatening."

"So why does she look like a bag of shit warmed up in an oven?" Sarah asked.

"Fever from the infection."

Sarah pouted. "Poor thing."

"We'll have to get her a card," Howard said.

"Screw you," Ashley spat at them.

Palu walked to the foot of Ashley's bed and looked her over.

Ashley pulled the blanket aside. "Want to climb in with me, big boy? I've never gone *mocha* before."

Palu tilted his head. "What on earth happened to you, child? Has this world chewed you up and spat you out so badly? If so, I want you to know that I understand. Life can be so cruel. It can turn our hearts to stone before we even reach puberty. I know."

Ashley rolled her eyes. "You have no idea what you're talking about. You work for the Government. You make me sick."

"Perhaps you and I are not so different," Palu continued. "I'd like to tell you a story, Ashley. Would that be okay?"

Ashley rolled her eyes again. "Knock yourself out."

Palu sat on the bed. "When I was a young boy, twelve years old, I lived in the region of the Punjab. My family were Jat, a proud people of Sikh heritage. During British rule, we were considered a 'martial' race, born warriors, but my father was just a farmer. He tended the fields and kept goats. Some would say he was a man of peace, yet deep in his blood was a fighting spirit like all Jat. The year was 1984, and a woman I hadn't even heard of had just been assassinated in New Delhi by her Sikh bodyguards. The woman's name was Indira Gandhi, and she was Prime Minister of India. I was just a boy. I knew nothing of events outside my home or the small school I attended in the village."

Ashley feigned boredom. "When are you going to get to the good part?"

"After Indira Gandhi was murdered, there were many troubles in India. Because the perpetrators were Sikh, the Hindus of India felt the assassination had been a conspiracy by our people. In the towns and cities, Sikh men and women were attacked in the streets, beaten to death by angry mobs. I could see the anxiety on my father's face growing each day as he continued to work the fields, but he assured us that the violence would not reach our quiet, little farm. He was wrong. My father's farm was large, and one of few in the region. Some of our Hindu neighbours found opportunity in crisis. They stirred up hatred in the village, blamed Sikhs for the death of their beloved Prime Minister, and pointed fingers at our family. Soon, there was a mob at our door. My father locked my mother and me inside and then went to talk sense into our neighbours and friends who had known him for years. I do not know what my father said to them. All I know is that they beat my father into a coma and set fire to our farm. I saw it all. Later that night they beat me too and took my mother to the bedroom where she screamed all night."

Sarah swallowed. Her stomach hurt hearing Palu's tale of misery and injustice.

Palu finished his story, seeming unmoved by it, as if he had replayed it a hundred times in his head. "My father died in hospital a week later. Our farm was purchased by our neighbours for practically nothing. I was sent to Britain to live with my uncle. Two years later, I was due to return to India, but I received news that my mother had killed herself. I had not seen her since the night the mob had come for us. So you see, Ashley, you are not the only one who feels betrayed and angry.

I watched my neighbors destroy my home and family while my Government did nothing to stop it. The men responsible were never punished. My blood boils at the thought of it, but I have not repeated the cycle of violence. I have not allowed my anger to manifest and spread. I chose a different path. Ashley, you need to choose a different path, too. Help us ensure there are no more attacks. Innocent people get hurt when you sow hatred, and it needs to stop. Do you understand?"

"I can't help you. It's too late."

"What do you mean?" Sarah asked.

Ashley cleared her throat and looked at them like they were idiots. "This is more than just a few suicide vests. This whole country will come crumbling down. By the end of this, there will be no more United Kingdom."

"Please explain," Palu said. From the way Ashley looked at him, it was clear he held her respect more than anybody else in the room. "Is this because of a man named Wazir Hesbani? Do you know where he is? How do you know Dr Cartwright?"

Ashley chuckled. "Cartwright? My dad hired the chubby fool after my brother died. Hesbani reached out to us through him."

"Where is Hesbani now?" Sarah demanded.

He is everywhere. Don't you feel him? His shadow is looming over this country like a plague. Before this is over, people will be too afraid to leave their homes. They'll forget about their cars, their jobs, their gluttonous shopping sprees. People will be reminded of what matters, what is truly valuable: life. People need to respect life before we have any hope of changing."

Sarah folded her arms. The girl sounded just like Al-Sharir. They still didn't know if the man was involved in this. "And you think the way to make people respect life is through violence? Don't you find that a little hypocritical? I think your whole argument falls apart when you get to the indiscriminate killing part."

"Sometimes death is the only way to ensure life. What time is it?"

Sarah sneered in disgust. "Why are you involved in this, Ashley? What did your mother and father die for? This can't all be because the Government bulldozed your house and moved your brother's body."

Ashley's face crinkled up in anger. "You're damn right it's not. Taking the home where I grew up, where my little brother played before he died, was just the first thing they did to us. I asked what time it is."

Sarah checked her watch. "It's 12.30PM. What do you mean? What did the Government do to you?"

"When my dad put up a fight and started a petition to stop the HS2 link, the government blacklisted his construction company. Suddenly my father lost all of his civil contracts. No more new-build homes, no more municipal structures, no more maintenance contracts. The taxman wanted to investigate his every movement, too. They ground my father's business to a halt with red tape—his livelihood of over thirty years gone almost overnight. If the Government is willing to do that to a hardworking, law-abiding family man, they've lost their right to be in charge."

"Looked like you were doing all right to me," Howard said. "Your new home was a nice place to live. Did you buy it with the fair settlement you got from the Government?"

"Fair settlement? Are you kidding? We got half what the house was worth. They screwed the figures and valued it based on what it cost my dad to build it thirty years ago. It was nowhere near what the house was worth on the current market. The house we moved to is rented. My father's company is due to go bankrupt within the month. They took everything from us, just so people can get to London a few minutes faster on the train. Business and shopping—that's what my family's entire life was destroyed for."

Ashley's sob story didn't excuse what she'd done. "Where is Hesbani?" Sarah demanded again. "I heard his goddamn voice on your father's answering machine, so don't lie to me. Where do I find him?"

"He'll find you. What you people need to worry about now is the next suicide bomb. There's going to be an explosion in less than two hours."

"Where?" Palu asked, still perching on the bed. "Ashley, this is important. This is your chance to undo some of what you've done. We can help you if you help us."

Ashley looked like she was going to cry, but then she surprised them all by laughing. "I don't want to help you. I want you all to burn."

Palu's caring demeanour disappeared. He stood from the bed, turned his back on Ashley, and straightened his tie. Then he spun around and smashed his fist on the bed sheets, right where Ashley's wounded foot lay.

Ashley bellowed.

Palu ripped off the sheets and grabbed the girl's wounded hand. He squeezed. "Tell me where the next target is!"

Ashley screamed.

Dr Bennett gasped. "Director Palu!"

"What is the next target? Tell me, or I'll start taking fingers."

Ashley wailed in agony. Palu slapped her, then gave her a chance to speak.

"T-the answering machine. It's... it's orders for the next target."

Palu eased up. "What do you mean? Sarah, what did you say about an answering machine message?"

Sarah thought back. "It was Hesbani. He said that two freedom fighters had been killed in Syria by the British."

"What does it mean?" Palu demanded of Ashley.

"It's an eye for an eye," said Bradley. "In the second videotape, Hesbani warned that for every life taken on foreign soil, we would lose just as many back home."

"What does that tell us?" Howard asked. "Two freedom fighters will be killed in the UK?"

"Law enforcement," Sarah said. "They're going to hit our police officers."

Ashley grinned. "Tick tock, bitches."

Sarah struck Ashely with a backhand blow. Blood trickled from the corner of the girl's mouth, but she continued grinning. Sarah pulled the SIG from her waistband and pressed it against Ashley's forehead. "Tick tock, bitch. Three seconds 'till I smear your brains on the pillow. Where is the bomb?"

Ashley closed her eyes and waited. Three seconds passed and Sarah didn't pull the trigger. The bluff hadn't worked. Ashley was prepared to die. Sarah lowered her weapon and sighed. "There's nothing left in you but hate, is there?"

Ashley opened her eyes. "You want to kill me, then do it. I'll never help you, and you'll never stop Hesbani. His plan is too far in motion. I set the latest bomb myself. You'll never find it."

Sarah put her gun away and wiped the sweat from her forehead. The group moved far enough away from Ashley that they could speak in private. "We need to go back to the Foster's residence. If Ashley made the bomb herself, that might be where she did it."

Howard agreed. "Especially if it was recent. We found her hiding out there this morning. Come on, let's go."

"You sure you can manage with the arm?" Sarah asked.

Howard held up his cast. "You can sign it once we stop Hesbani."

"Deal."

"Okay," Palu said. "Sarah, Howard, get back to the Foster's home. I'll have Mattock meet you there."

"What about Mandy?" Howard said.

"Mattock will leave one of his men at the hospital. I'll keep working the leads, try to figure out where the likeliest target will be." Palu pointed a finger at Ashley. "Bradley, you and Dr Bennet stay here and get what you can from her."

Everyone agreed on the plan and got going. Before Sarah left the room, Ashley grinned and said, "Tick tock, tick tock."

17

JACK IN THE BOX

Despite Sarah breaking every speed limit on the way to the Foster's home, Mattock was still there before her and Howard. His Range Rover, identical to the ones back at MCU, was parked up on the curb waiting for them.

Mattock joined them on the driveway once they were ready. "Neighbours have eyes on us," he said.

"They were woken by gunshots this morning. I'm not surprised," Howard said.

Sarah nodded at the police tape across the property's front door. "Are the police still here?"

Mattock stared up the driveway. "No, I had them called off for a couple hours."

Sarah raised an eyebrow. "We can do that?"

"Not often, but we have some clout when we need it. We get authorisation through the Home Office directly."

Sarah and Howard followed Mattock inside the house. Leanne Foster's body had been removed, but her blood remained on the tiles and spattered on the kitchen cupboards. Sarah felt sick by the sight of it.

"What are we looking for?" Mattock asked, unaffected by the scene.

Sarah opened drawers, looking for paperwork, IDs, anything. "There's another suicide bomb, and it's going to go off soon. Ashley isn't talking, so we need to figure this out ourselves. We're searching for clues, anything that might tell us who or what's involved."

Mattock clenched his jaw. "Bleeding nutcases, the lot of 'em. Ain't never seen anything like this—normal families turning to terrorism."

"We can figure out the whys later," Howard said. "We need to turn this place over quickly."

Mattock nodded. "I'll check upstairs."

Sarah and Howard took the back of the house first. The kitchen and study were a bust. That left the lounge and dining room at the front of the house.

Howard checked the dining room while Sarah took the lounge. Each wall held multiple pictures of the Fosters holding hands, hugging, and otherwise posing for the camera. They looked happy. Sarah also noticed that the home in most of the pictures was not the one she was standing in. A picture on a side table showed a quaint, extended cottage with timber beams and white walls. It had a double garage and a giant front lawn. On the front lawn was a bouncy castle with a grinning infant who must have been Ashley's brother.

Other than the photographs, the living room was bare and fashionable, with few knickknacks or surfaces to accumulate dust. An LCD television hung on the wall in front of a leather sofa that had two small tables on either side.

There was a chest of drawers against the back wall which was the only place left to search, but before Sarah got chance, Mattock rushed into the room looking concerned. "You need to see this," he said.

Sarah grabbed Howard and they went upstairs following Mattock. "I think it's the girl's room," he told them. "It's a mess."

Sarah walked into Ashley's bedroom, and the coppery smell of blood hit her. There was too much of it to all belong to Dr Cartwright, who was slumped against the far wall beside the bed. A bullet hole marked his temple.

Howard knelt in front of the body. "Why did they take out the doc after having rescued him?"

"Maybe he had cold feet after what happened at the clinic," Sarah suggested. "He seemed to have doubts about what they were doing. Maybe his conscience finally kicked in."

Mattock nodded to the bed. "Or maybe Ashley had one last job for Cartwright before he became expendable."

Dried blood caked Ashley's bed. Crumpled towels and bowls of bloody water sat on the bedside tables. At the foot of the bed was an open medical kit.

"Cartwright was a surgeon before he was a therapist," Sarah noted.

"He must have fixed Ashley's wounds after the shootout," Howard said. "Bradley shot her."

"No, this is more than that. There's too much blood for just a hand wound."

"What are you thinking?" Mattock asked.

"I'm not sure yet." Sarah knelt over the medical kit and rooted through its contents. There were bandages and gauze as well as a bloody scalpel and sutures. There was also an empty vial of iodine. The strangest thing inside the bag was an empty box of condoms.

"What have you got?" Howard asked.

Sarah sighed and tried to make sense of things. "I think Cartwright cut Ashley open."

Howard frowned. "But why?"

Mattock picked up a coil of bloodstained electrical wire from the windowsill. "I think maybe this has something to do with it."

Sarah's stomach ached as she placed it all together. "It's inside of her! Dr Cartwright cut Ashley open and placed a goddamn bomb inside of her!"

"No way," Howard said.

"Sounds a bit far-fetched, luv," said Mattock.

But Sarah was sure. "Ashley must've killed the doctor after he was through, making sure he wouldn't get a chance to feel guilty and talk. They rigged a bomb together, something small and compact, like C4, and then Ashley wrapped it in condoms while Cartwright inserted it in her. Ashley is the suicide bomber, I'm certain of it."

Sarah leapt to her feet and yanked out her mob-sat. "Palu? Ashley is the suicide bomber. The bomb is inside her. You need to—"

Sarah's mouth dropped open and the mob-sat slipped from her grasp, landing amongst the bloody bandages on the floor.

Mattock and Howard stared at her, waiting for her to speak.

"We need to get back," she said. "I think the Earthworm just exploded."

18

SPINNING TOP

Howard called MCU a dozen times on the frantic trip back to the Earthworm. Sarah and Mattock both drove 120mph down the dual carriageway, Range Rover following Jaguar. Several times Sarah thought she might crash, but she couldn't slow down. Not until she reached the Earthworm and saw things for herself.

As soon as they reached the derelict farm, Sarah knew the worst had happened. A flume of black smoke billowed from the middle of the open field, coming from some burning structure beneath the ground.

Howard opened the concealed entrance and they beat it down the steps as fast as they could. Nobody spoke, the anticipation too much to put into words.

As they reached the lower steps, they heard the blood-curdling siren.

"It's the evacuation alarm," Howard shouted over the din. He entered the entry code for the hatch into the tail section.

Inside, the only light came from the red strobe lights of the alarm system and the strip lighting that illuminated the floor. They sprinted through the large unused tail section and made it over to the other side, fearful of what they would find. As soon as Howard opened the next hatch, the epicentre of destruction became clear.

The smoke billowed out at them in angry clouds. Sarah covered her mouth and tried not to choke on it. Mattock unclipped something from his belt and threw it into the hallway. It was a glow stick and, as it snapped to life, it bathed everything in a soft green glow.

Howard shouted into the smoke. There was a weak reply somewhere off down the hallway. Sarah didn't hang around but took off into the black haze.

It was impossible to see, and she had to grope her way along the wall, using the yelping voice as a guide. "Palu? Is that you? Where are you?"

"I'm here," the director moaned. "Keep moving forward."

Sarah found Palu slumped in the hallway, caked in soot and breathing into his scrunched up tie. Blood poured from a thick gash on his forehead, but he otherwise looked okay.

Sarah knelt in front of him. "You okay?"

"I don't know what happened."

"The bomb was inside Ashley. She was the next suicide bomber. We were the freedom fighters she meant to hit."

"You mean they planned this all along?"

Sarah shrugged. "I don't know. Dr Cartwright sewed the bomb inside of her and he's dead."

Palu dragged himself up off the floor, but winced and slid back down. "Then we have nothing. All our leads are gone."

Sarah put an arm around the man's waist and helped him to his feet. Soon, Howard and Mattock joined her and helped her get out of the smoke, back into the tail section. There, they dumped Palu in one of the dusty seats and took a moment to clear their throats.

"Palu?" said Howard. "I'm glad you're okay. Where are Bradley and Dr Bennett?"

"They were in the infirmary with Ashley."

"We need to go back," Sarah said.

Palu shook his head. "You need to wait for the smoke to clear. The sprinklers kicked in and dealt with the fire, but it will take a while for the extractors to clear the air."

Sarah flopped on a chair and let her chin fall to her chest. "This just keeps getting worse."

They all waited until the smoke cleared enough to tolerate. Then Sarah, Howard, and Mattock sprinted down the hallway towards the infirmary, choking on what was left of the smoky air. Palu stayed behind, still catching his breath.

At the infirmary, they were met by a smattering of dying fires. Ceiling sprinklers had kept the flames contained, but the damage from the blast had gone unanswered.

The infirmary was nothing but a black smudge. The tiles had cracked from the heat, and the furniture had smashed against the walls. In the middle of the floor was a wet, lumpy mess that had once been Ashley Foster.

Movement caught Sarah's eye and she spotted Dr Bennett on the floor, alive.

"Jessica?" she said. "Jessica, it's okay."

Bennett was on her knees in the corner, hunched over somebody and performing CPR. She was moaning and sobbing as she did so.

Sarah walked towards her.

Bradley was dead.

Even with Bennett performing CPR, it was obvious he wasn't coming back. His face was an unrecognisable mess, but his bright blue eyes gave him away. One of his ribs jutted out of his torso at a right angle.

Sarah moved up to the doctor and placed a hand on her

shoulder. It made her flinch, but she continued performing CPR. "Hey, doc," she said. "Let's get you out of here. There's nothing you can do."

Bennett stopped pumping and looked up at Sarah, tears in her eyes. She allowed herself to be helped to her feet, but after two unsteady steps, she fell weeping into Sarah's arms. Sarah held the woman and patted her back.

After a few minutes had passed, Sarah carried Dr Bennett out of the infirmary. Mattock and Howard stayed behind with Bradley, both of them utterly gob smacked. In the corridor, Dr Bennett managed to stop crying for a moment. She produced a handkerchief and wiped away some of the soot from her face. "I don't understand it," she said. "How did Ashley get a bomb in here?"

"It was inside her," Sarah explained. "Did she have any recently stitched wounds when you examined her?"

"The girl was covered in wounds, head to toe. I had no reason to think..."

Sarah patted her shoulder. "None of us knew. This whole thing has been impossible to predict from the start."

"No, it hasn't," Bennett spat. "Bradley getting hurt was very easy to predict. He was going to leave MCU because he *knew* this was too much for him. *You* stopped him from leaving. His death is on your hands."

Sarah wanted to argue, but Bennett was right. Bradley was dead because she had made him stay. The kid had never been cut out for this.

But that wasn't true, was it? Sarah and Bradley had taken down Ashley Foster together. Bradley was a good soldier, and he had wanted to fight the good fight.

"I'm sorry, Jessica," said Sarah.

Bennett shook her head, fought off another wave of tears,

and then marched down the hallway on her own, disappearing.

"You okay?" Palu asked her, coming back from the empty tail section.

"No," Sarah said. "Not at all."

She went back into the infirmary, where Mattock and Howard were on the floor beside Bradley. The smoke had cleared, and the scene would have looked a little less like a nightmare if not for the blood and bodies.

Sarah joined Mattock and Howard on the floor. She thought about how Bradley had compared her to a Jack Russell Terrier. He'd been right about her from the very beginning and had stuck up for her all the way. She'd almost made a friend, but nothing had changed in the end. Sarah was still the same person she had been when all of this began. She should never have let herself give a damn. This was her reward for caring.

Trusting people was never worth the risk. Every time Sarah let herself care for somebody, they died. Her mother, Thomas, Miller, Hamish, her baby, and now Bradley. If it wasn't for Howard dragging her into all this, she would be alone, safe, and unbothered. The world was too shitty a place to get involved in.

She was done. As soon as she was on her feet she was walking out of this God-forsaken place and never looking back. She just needed to rest first, sit for a while and think.

AFGHANISTAN, 2008

Sarah sat, staring out the window as the banged-up Corolla bounced across the sand flats. The doors rattled in their rusty fixtures, and grains of sand made it in around the loose edges. Every time Sarah bit down, she was met with a jarring crunch of sand between her teeth.

They told her they were taking her back to camp as promised. Al-Sharir sat upfront with Hesbani, and two other men guarded Sarah in the back with AK47s across their laps.

After they slaughtered Hamish, Sarah gave up any hope of getting home alive. Her hand stayed on her belly, and she tried not to weep as she thought about how she'd failed her unborn child. It was her job to protect it. It had been her job to protect Hamish and her other men, too, but she had failed at every turn. She would go to Hell, she was sure.

They drove for two hours, the banged-up Corolla managing only 40mph. Sarah looked out the window and tried to spot landmarks, but there were none. Camp Bastion was isolated in the desert, impossible to sneak up on from any direction. That was why Sarah knew she wasn't being taken there. If the Corolla came within five miles of the camp, Al-Sharir and his men would be seized. They were just looking for a good spot to bury her.

The Corolla's gears crunched as they slowed. Al-Sharir and Hesbani exchanged heated words up front, but Sarah couldn't translate quickly enough to get the gist. All she knew was that they were disagreeing.

The car came to a stop, and the two men with AK47s pulled Sarah out. She fell onto her hands and knees before leaping back up on her feet. Hesbani was right there to shove her away from the car. The men with the AKs aimed at her, but Sarah didn't put her hands up. If they were going to kill her, there was nothing she could do about it, so why beg?

Hesbani was sneering at her.

"You're a bunch of monsters," she shouted, spitting into the sand.

Al-Sharir stood before her, calm as always. "I guarantee,

Captain, if our countries were to count bodies, yours would win. You judge us by standards your own people fail to uphold."

Sarah didn't respond. Al-Sharir was probably right, but that didn't make what he was doing acceptable. He spoke about ending violence, yet he exercised it as freely as the Taliban did.

"You gave me your word you would let me go," she said, looking him in the eye.

"Words mean nothing to the West," Hesbani snarled. "You English shake hands in friendship with your left while picking our pockets with your right, all the while hiding missile behind your back. I will not rest until I see your people in ruins as you seek to see ours."

"We want to help you," Sarah said for the final time. "Say what you want about my country, but you don't speak for me, you son-of-a-bitch. I wanted to help you people, but now you can all just suck my dick."

Hesbani seemed confused by the insult, but Al-Sharir smiled. "You are a warrior, Captain. True of heart and ignorant of fear. Allah protects those who are true to their beliefs. May he keep you safe now."

Sarah waited for the bullet.

The AKs stayed pointed at her, but Al-Sharir didn't give the order to kill her. Instead he smiled at her and said, "You may leave now, Captain. Your Camp Bastion is ten miles in that direction," he pointed. "It is hot, and you are tired and injured. It is more likely that you will die, but if you are with child, as you say, Allah will watch over you and you will make it. Do not take up arms against my people again, or there will be great consequences. I could have killed you, but did not, so your pledge to no-violence is not optional. You owe your life to me and all that you do with it."

Sarah couldn't believe it. She stared across the empty desert at the unreachable horizon. If she could keep walking in a straight line, she might find Camp Bastion, but if she veered even slightly off course, she'd miss it by a mile and die in the dirt.

"Teach your child to respect Allah," Hesbani shouted after her as she walked away. "Or I will cut his throat the same as I cut your Corporal's throat."

Sarah almost ran to claw out Hesbani's eyes. She hated herself for walking away from the man who'd killed her squad and scarred her face, but she wanted to live. She was a coward.

Sarah managed a dozen steps before she looked back. Not only were the men not following her, but they were climbing back inside the Corolla. When they sped off in the opposite direction, Sarah let out a deep sigh of relief and cried. She cried for hours.

Night fell by the time her legs gave out. She might have walked twenty miles, but in the desert, it was impossible to tell. When she finally stopped for a rest, tumbling to her hands and knees, the scorching sand had gone frigid. Soon, she would be shivering and succumbing to the chill, with no place to take shelter.

She needed to get moving. Her entire body ached, but there was no longer any pain coming from her wounded thigh or her ruined face. She was numb from the head down, and dog-tired. She tried to get up, but couldn't, so opted to crawl, but she ended up falling onto her belly as her elbows folded in on themselves. Her father would have gloated. She was exactly like what he had said all women were, weak and far too delicate. She didn't have what it took to survive in a world run by men.

I'm sorry, she told her unborn child. *I'm sorry,* she told her husband Thomas. *I can't do it.*

Sarah did not try to get up again. The pain of trying to live was too great. She had earned her chance to rest, even if it would be everlasting.

When a routine patrol passed by, she heard the rumbling engine of their Snatch-2, but couldn't lift her head and look for them.

If not for the thermal imaging goggles, the squad's signalman was wearing, they would have driven right by her. Instead, just twenty minutes later, Sarah found herself inside Camp Bastion, with a doctor working away on her. She held her tummy and thanked God.

19

DIABLO

Palu re-entered the ruined infirmary several hours later to get everyone. The room was an unsafe mess, and it wasn't doing anyone any good hanging around there.

Sarah's eyes had focused on Bradley's body for so long, they felt crusty when she turned them upwards to see Palu.

"What is it, Boss?" Mattock asked.

Palu's face sagged. Despite having cleaned himself up, he looked to have aged ten years. "There's been another video," he said.

Howard climbed to his feet, trying not to lean on his cast. "Shab Bekhier?"

"Yes, the same three men as before, with Hesbani as the mouthpiece, as usual. I have it ready to view in the conference room. Fortunately, our systems are all still operational, and the main power is back on. The damage is confined to the infirmary, so we need to move out of here."

Mattock hopped to his feet. "Let's go watch this video then. We need to find Hesbani and put an end to this fucking circus."

Howard offered Sarah his hand. "You coming?"

She stepped away. "You guys go. I'm out."

He looked at her and frowned. "What do you mean, you're out?"

"I'm not cut out for this. All I've done is screw up, and now Bradley is dead."

"That isn't your fault, Captain," Mattock told her.

"Isn't it? Seems all I've ever done is guide people to their deaths. I can't take it anymore."

"I don't have time for this," Palu said. "I'll be waiting in the conference room, everybody ready to go in five minutes."

Howard and Mattock rounded on Sarah. "You're wasting time," she told them both. "Just go."

Howard shook his head. "Whether you like it or not, you're a part of this, Sarah. You've bled with the rest of us, and you need to see this through to the end."

"Bradley died because of me."

"Bradley respected you. He died because you made him believe in himself; nobody here could manage that. We need you on this team."

"What team? There's not enough of you to play five-a-side football."

"Exactly," Mattock said. "The last thing we need is you scarpering. If you think people have died because of you, the only way you'll ever get that blood off your hands is by stopping people like Hesbani. Bradley died for this team. Don't slap his memory in the face by quitting. He had the balls to stay. Do you?"

Sarah stared at Bradley. The kid had brought out a maternal instinct in Sarah that she'd lost long ago. That instinct was lost because of Hesbani. He had ruined her life three years ago, and he was still ruining it today.

Sarah remembered lying face down in the desert. She

remembered how Hesbani had crushed her spirits in the heat of Afghanistan. It was time to find her way out of that desert and stop being afraid.

Sarah took Howard's hand. "Okay," she said. "I'll stay in this thing until Hesbani is finished. Then I'm gone."

Howard nodded. "You help us find Hesbani, and I'll personally drive you to your doorstep and never bother you again."

"Sounds perfect. Come on, we've got a video to watch."

"I'll bring the popcorn," Mattock said.

They set off to the conference room where they found Dr Bennet and Palu already waiting. Bennett looked upset when she saw Sarah, and for a second, it looked like she would kick up a fuss. Instead, she nodded and said, "Glad we're all here. Bradley would want us to stick together."

Sarah nodded at Bennett and sat down at the table.

Palu wasted no time. "This was posted on ClipShare ten minutes ago. Hesbani must have known Ashley Foster's plan to blow herself up."

"How?" Howard asked. "Nobody knows MCU exists."

"I don't think we were the target," Palu told them. "The plan was to hit whoever took Ashley into custody. We weren't the specific target: the whole of law enforcement was."

"What do you mean?" asked Sarah. "Who else was hit?"

Palu pressed play without another word.

Hesbani and two other men appeared on screen again. Sarah was becoming surer that one of the three men was white. Like everything else, it made little sense. Hesbani would never work with a non-Muslim, Sarah was sure. The third person stayed near the back. They were of slight build and had only their dark eyes on display. Their shorter height suggested they weren't yet fully grown—or female.

It was impossible to tell whether the video had been at

night or during the day, but the ceiling's light source was rocking to-and-fro like it had in both the previous videos.

"United Kingdom, you have been warned," Hesbani said, "yet you continue on your path of arrogance and hatred. Two freedom fighters in Islamic Syria were killed this morning by British soldiers. Shab Bakhier pledged to you that blood would be met with blood. In response to your wanton murder of these innocent Syrians, we have struck at your own freedom fighters. More deaths will occur if Prime Minister Breslow does not recall your nation's troops from foreign soil. Today saw the death of more of Allah's martyrs. Paul, Leanne, and Ashley Foster died today, trying to save you from yourselves. They are by Allah's side now, reaping their eternal rewards. These are your final moments, Britain. Have your Prime Minister seek forgiveness now, or watch your crooked empire burn to the ground."

There was silence for a moment as the video ended.

"Four police officers were killed outside Scotland Yard this morning," explained Palu. "Hit by a sniper. Early reports suggest that a van pulled up at the end of the road and the shooter fired through an open window. The attack took less than five-seconds."

"Only a pro could hit four targets on a horizontal plane in five-seconds," said Mattock. "Does Hesbani have any military connections?"

Palu shook his head. "Only with the Taliban, and they aren't known for their marksmanship."

"With Ashley Foster dead," said Howard, "where do we have to go from here?"

"I'm not sure," Palu admitted. "Thames Valley Police are going through the Foster's home and business right now. Police Commissioner Howe will keep me updated. Home Office have briefed him fully on our operation."

"And until then?" Sarah asked. "We just wait, after what they did to Bradley and Mandy?"

"Did you see anything in the video that could help?" Dr Bennett asked her, staying on task.

Sarah thought. "It was the same location as before. No window, no landmarks. Just a table, a lamp, and a swinging light bulb above them."

"What about the men in the video?" Howard asked.

"I'm convinced one of them is white."

"Perhaps he's the sniper," Mattock suggested. "Maybe they have a British soldier in their ranks. Wouldn't be the first time somebody has flipped."

Sarah wondered what could make a person terrorise their own country, but couldn't understand it.

Bennett leaned against the table and sighed. "What about Bradley?"

"What about him?" said Howard.

"Before he went to pick up Sarah, he was working on a lead. Did he get anything?"

Palu nodded at Bradley's laptop, still sitting open on the table. "I'm not sure. He was tracking the owner of the newsagent, the Pakistani immigrant. I don't know if he found anything."

Dr Bennett moved in front of Bradley's laptop and began typing. "Looks like he was researching land registry and property records for a Mr Hamil Hamidi."

Palu nodded. "That's the owner of the newsagent."

"Maybe it's Hesbani's alias," suggested Howard.

"What about the niece?" Sarah asked. "Didn't we find out that the newsagent is run by a niece?"

Bennett nodded. "Aziza Hamidi. There's nothing on her here except her employment records at the newsagent. It doesn't look like Bradley managed to... no, wait."

Palu leaned forward. "What is it?"

"One second." Bennett zipped a file onto the large television screen.

"What we looking at?" Mattock asked.

"Bradley compiled a list of all properties registered to Hamil Hamidi."

They took a moment to examine the list. Sarah spotted the Oxfordshire newsagent and multiple other businesses, ranging from a florist to a Halal slaughterhouse. Whoever Hamil Hamidi was, he was well-heeled with a seemingly endless range of investments. One item on the list particularly caught Sarah's attention: a listed building, described as derelict. It wasn't so much the building that piqued her interest, so much as the address: Thornton Cross Station House (Derelict, Class 2 listed building), 1 Station Road, Redditch. "He owns a property next to a train station. The videos all had an unstable light source, like a bulb swinging."

Howard looked at her. "Caused by the vibrations of trains coming in and out of the station?"

Sarah nodded. "It's likely that's where Hesbani is making the videos."

"Then that's where we'll find him," Mattock said. "And we can finally kick his bloody arse."

"That's going to be all me," Sarah said. "And God help anybody who gets in my way."

She was scared shitless, but she knew that the only way she would ever get any peace was by facing Hesbani, and then taking the son-of-a-bitch down.

Palu folded his arms and moved back in his chair. "So you're back with us then, Captain?"

"You're damn right I am, and it's Sarah."

Palu smiled. "Glad to have you with us, Sarah."

"Well," Mattock said, "guess that's the team talk over. Shall we make a move?"

Sarah stood up. "I'm driving."

20

NEW HOPE

Despite the town of Redditch being close to her flat in Moseley, Sarah hadn't visited before. It was just another Birmingham satellite town. Patches of parkland shoved up against industrial sections to disguise them, and residential estates centred around small shopping hubs called 'centres,' but despite the annoying amount of roundabouts and ring roads, the town was pretty. Sarah spotted signs for both a lake and an abbey, and they passed several playing fields full of children.

It was now Wednesday morning, and Sarah couldn't believe how little sleep she could operate on. It was like having cotton wool inside her skull, but somehow she felt more alert and focused than ever.

She pulled off the highway and onto the ring road that would take them into Redditch's town centre. There were signs indicating the rail station was ahead. Sarah reported in, fiddling with the steering wheel's controls to reach Palu. "We're in Redditch," she told him. "Just heading to the station now."

"I've put the local police on alert," Palu informed her.

"They'll be nearby if you need backup. They've been informed that you're an anti-terrorist task force working under the purview of the Met."

"Roger that," Howard said from the passenger seat. "Permission to use force if necessary?"

"Lethal force granted, but know that you will be operating in the centre of a civilian area. There can be absolutely no collateral damage. I want every bullet accounted for."

"I'll beat Hesbani to death with his own shoes if I have to," said Sarah. "No need for bullets."

"Keep me updated." Palu signed off.

Mattock was chuckling to himself. "You know, Sarah, you have quite the sick sense of humour. Reminds me of someone I know."

Sarah clenched the wheel. "If you mean my father, I don't want to hear it."

"Fair enough."

Howard looked at her, but she refused to make eye-contact. "You okay?"

"I'm fine. I just can't go into… that."

They came up by a courthouse and a glass-fronted college and continued following signs for the rail station. They found it opposite an open-air bus depot.

"That must be it," Mattock said, pointing to a large Georgian house right next to the station. "It's a derelict building, right? That place looks pretty derelict."

Sarah pulled into the station's car park, and they got out the moment the engine died. The station platform was deserted, no doubt because of the terrorism alert.

Sarah, Mattock, and Howard wore the luminous yellow jackets of workmen. People paid workmen no mind, especially when it came to derelict buildings.

The new rail station had been placed directly in front of

the old one. They couldn't enter the fenced-off area of the derelict station without crossing over the tracks. The front of the building was blocked by the elevated ring road.

Howard cleared his throat. "Any ideas on how we get in?"

Sarah looked around. "If Hesbani is using this place, there must be a way in and out. He wouldn't climb the fence in front of a station full of people."

"What about there?" Mattock pointed at an office block adjacent to the rear of the derelict station house.

Sarah nodded. "Let's check it out."

They found a footpath and headed around the new train station towards the old. They came out around the opposite side and were heading towards the office block. When they got there, they found it abandoned as well. Not derelict, but vacant and FOR RENT. The office block was empty and private.

"This must be it," Sarah said. "Let's keep our heads low and find a way through."

They crept up to the office building, looking about themselves for the slightest movement. There were people working in other offices across the road, and there was a driving test centre nearby, but nobody was paying any attention to them. The yellow workmen jackets were doing their job.

"What about here?" Mattock said. He was standing by a gated alleyway at the side of the vacant office building.

"Is the gate unlocked?" Sarah asked.

Mattock grabbed the lock and twisted it. The metal gate creaked open.

Sarah and Howard looked at one another as Mattock slipped into the alleyway and disappeared. Things were going smoother than expected.

They kept their heads down and followed the pathway into a yard. A chain link fence separated the office plot from the derelict station house. There was a wide tear in the bottom of the steel mesh.

Sarah was sure no one on the platform could see them. "Okay," she said, "guns out."

Mattock took point. His gun was the biggest, and he looked the least likely of them to die from a gunshot wound to the face. He stepped through the gap in the fence and moved into the grounds of the old station house. Sarah went through after him, followed by Howard. They all watched the boarded windows, wary of anything lurking behind them.

Was Hesbani inside? Sarah wasn't sure how she would react if he was. Hesbani had haunted her dreams for six years, and the thought of meeting him face to face was like meeting the bogeyman.

The derelict station's doorframe was rotten, brown, and splintered. When Mattock shoved up against it, the door swung aside easily, scraping across the stone floor as it hung from warped hinges.

There was nothing inside but darkness.

Sarah stepped inside and flinched as fallen masonry crunched underfoot. There were old fare tickets and route maps fading against the stone floor like carpet.

"Looks like it's ready to crumble any minute," Howard whispered. "Why haven't they demolished it already?"

"Because somebody owns it," Sarah said. "Whoever this Hamil Hamidi is, he obviously wants the place standing."

They checked out all the side rooms, but found nothing. Now they needed to check the upper floors. They congregated in front of the house's grand staircase and looked upwards.

"I'm not sure trying to climb that thing is a sound idea," Mattock said. "Bloody thing's falling apart."

"It's just a bit of peeling paint."

She took the first step, SIG pointed up the stairs. Howard

and Mattock followed closely behind. Dust puffed out from beneath their boots as they disturbed thick piles. It looked like nobody had come through here in years, but there were tell-tale signs that that wasn't true. Sarah noticed a few places on each step where the stone showed through the dust—recent footsteps.

At the top, the rooms on each side were open-fronted and wide, the interiors gutted with no way to tell what had once stood inside them.

Mattock tutted. "This floor is a bust."

Sarah ground her teeth. They couldn't afford not to find anything here. It was the only solid lead they had.

She made for the next set of stairs and started upwards. Howard and Mattock hissed at her to be cautious, but she left them with no option but to follow.

When they reached the third and final floor, Sarah grinned. "Found you."

The entire third floor was open-plan. It'd been completely cleared of debris, and in its place was a line of desks and wall-mounted corkboards—the corkboards covered with detailed drawings of bombs, inked maps, and creased letters. It was an empty hive, left behind by its evacuating worker bees.

In the centre of the room was a video camera, perched atop a tripod and pointing at a bare desk with a single lamp plugged into a double power outlet. As a train departed the nearby station, Sarah looked up and saw a bare bulb swinging back and forth.

"You were right," said Howard, coming up behind Sarah. "Hesbani was here."

Sarah went to the nearest desk and plucked a photograph from the corkboard. It was a psychiatric report on Caroline Pugh, with Dr Cartwright's signature on the bottom. Paper-clipped to the back was a flyer for the pub she blew up.

Sarah found similar files for Jeffrey Blanchfield and the people responsible for blowing up Dartmouth and Arborfield.

Howard examined the files too. "We should get these to the local police," he said. "They're still trying to identify the other bombers."

The Dartmouth bomber had detonated on the ferry and sunk beneath the waves. The police couldn't distinguish between the bomber and the victims. "We'll call it all in once we're done," she said. "First, I want to —" Her eyes settled on the far end of the corkboard. "Oh no." She ripped four pages off the board and held them up for Howard and Mattock. "These places haven't been hit yet." She leafed through the papers. Four more medical histories of seemingly normal people, four more villages yet to be devastated.

Howard grabbed the papers from her and took a look. "I'll call Palu. We need to move."

Blam!

Everyone hit the ground at the sound of the gunshot. Sarah ducked beneath one of the desks and aimed her SIG, but couldn't find a target.

Blam!

The desk above Sarah's head splintered. She dove out from beneath it and rolled to her feet.

Then she found a target.

Emerging from a defunct bathroom was a man in a balaclava. He held a pistol in each hand and was pointing them both at Sarah. Mattock and Howard leapt from cover and fired just in time to send the man running.

Sarah wasted no time going after the assailant. The man in the balaclava raced down the stairs, leaping the steps three at a time, but Sarah took them four at a time. The man was fast, but something had possessed Sarah that threatened to have her take flight. Blood pulsed in her temples and her whole body shuddered as her boots pounded the ground.

Howard and Mattock gave chase behind Sarah, but they had no chance of keeping up. Ahead, the balaclava man sped across the first floor. Sarah was gaining on him, but fell back when he let a couple of shots off at her. Sarah ducked inside one of the gutted shop fronts and fired back three times.

The balaclava man grunted

Sarah's last round had hit home, catching the target in his leg. He clutched at his thigh and cursed, but before Sarah could line up another shot, he straightened out and let rip with both guns. Howard and Mattock were forced to retreat back up the stairs. Sarah leapt inside the empty shop and waited.

Blam Blam Clink!

One of balaclava man's guns went dry, and he threw it to the floor. He still had ammunition in his other weapon, but instead of emptying it at Sarah, he limped off in a hurry.

Sarah slipped out of the store front and followed the man down the final flight of stairs. In his desperation, he could still keep up a decent pace. She chased the man out of the building and into the yard. Panicked screaming came from the nearby train platform. The handful of people waiting there had heard the gunshots.

"Don't fucking move," Sarah shouted. She'd caught up enough to take balaclava man's head off if she wanted to.

The man stopped, put his hands in the air, and faced Sarah. He still held his gun, but pointed it at the sky.

"Get on your knees," she ordered.

The man chuckled. "On a first date, lass?"

Sarah growled. "Do it!"

The man got on his knees, hands still raised in the air.

"Drop the gun."

"But then what would I have to shoot you with?"

Sarah glared.

"All right, all right, I hear yer." He dropped his gun, and Sarah kicked it away.

She stood in front of the man, wondering why he gave her such a strange feeling. Almost like they'd met before. Perhaps it was the accent. "Who are you?" she demanded.

The man shrugged. "See for yerself."

Sarah grabbed the top of the man's balaclava and ripped it away. The face that looked back at her was a ghost. "Hamish?" she spluttered.

"Aye," Hamish said, saluting. "Good to see yer again, Captain. It's been a wee while."

Sarah was so shocked to see Hamish that she was taken completely by surprise when he leapt up and clocked her in the jaw. Her vision was spinning as he snatched away her SIG and made a run for the alley.

21

RETURN OF THE JEDI

Sarah fell as Hamish escaped into the alley. There she remained; not because of the blow to her jaw, but because of the paralyzing shock. That couldn't have been Hamish. Sarah had watched him die. She'd *let* him die.

Howard and Mattock sprinted into the yard and helped Sarah to her feet. Howard grabbed her by the shoulders. "Sarah, are you okay?"

Sarah stared blankly and tried to speak, but couldn't. Mattock slapped her. "Wake up! The wanker's getting away!"

"He headed into the alley," said Sarah, snapping back into focus.

They took off into the alley and were just in time to watch Hamish jump into the side of a black van with a rear spoiler. Sarah could see a woman inside wearing a burka. She was kneeling behind something mounted inside the van.

"Get down!" Sarah dove back into the alley, dragging Howard and Mattock with her.

The woman in the burka fired a mounted PK machine gun at them, releasing a torrent of bullets so rapidly that the noise became an incessant drone.

"Bleeding 'ell," Mattock growled. "Who's firing a goddamn bulletchucker at us?"

Sarah peered around the corner and tried to make out who the woman was, but the burka hid her identity. When the woman spotted Sarah, she pivoted the machine gun at her. The brickwork next to Sarah's head exploded.

"Unidentified woman. Belt-loaded PK," Sarah yelled over the din.

Mattock spat. "Sod it. She could have a thousand rounds before she runs out."

"We're pinned down," said Howard.

Sarah knew that a PK was a heavy piece of machinery from the soviet era. Pivoting it from one side to another was a slow, arduous affair. If she could draw the woman's aim, she might create an opportunity for Mattock and Howard to return fire.

"I'm going to break cover," she said. "Soon as I start running, you'll have a couple seconds to take her out."

Howard grabbed her arm. "Don't be a nutter. You'll be cut to ribbons."

"Not if you do your job." She shrugged free of his grasp and sprinted out of the alleyway. There was no cover, no place to go. The machine gun fire hit the ground behind her, a rainfall of lead. If Howard and Mattock weren't quick enough, it would catch up to her and tear her to pieces.

The two men leapt out of the alleyway behind her and let rip. Sarah kept on sprinting, trying to keep ahead of the stream of death.

The machine gun stopped firing.

Sarah spun around and watched the woman in the burka dive inside the van for cover. Then she saw Hamish sliding the panel door shut behind them both. They were going to make a break for it.

The van backed up, its tyres skidding on the pavement. The unknown driver shifted into gear and swung the vehicle around. Sarah had no weapon, but she couldn't help herself—she ran after the van.

Howard and Mattock fired until their clips went dry.

There was no way to stop the van, it was going to get away. Sarah gave her legs everything she had, sprinting for the vehicle as it circled towards her. It was getting close enough to flatten her, but she kept on running.

As the van got closer, Sarah spotted the driver inside. She stood her ground, rooted to the pavement. Her jaw clenched, eyes narrowed.

Hesbani.

Hesbani glared back at her, picking up speed. His face held a mixture of anger and surprise. He was obviously stunned to see her, but not displeased.

As the van sped towards her, Sarah continued to stand her ground. She raised her right hand and extended her middle finger.

Just in time, she leapt aside and landed on her stomach, forced to watch as the van took off past her and escaped. She would destroy Hesbani if it was the last thing she did.

Hesbani probably thought he hadn't been identified by the authorities—he'd been using Al-Sharir's name after all—but he would realise now that he was known and wanted. There was to be no more clandestine plotting, no more hiding in the shadows, and no more self-indulgent videos. His face would be in the hands of every law enforcement agency in the UK. That would make him desperate and more dangerous.

Sarah leapt to her feet. Howard and Mattock were reloading their weapons behind her.

"You okay?" Mattock asked her, running up alongside her.

"I'm fine. We need to get back in that building and rip it

apart for evidence. Hesbani's on the run now. We only have a small window of time before he disappears."

The sound of police sirens filled the air. "You and Howard get back inside the station house," Mattock said. "I'll clear things with the Old Bill as best I can. They ain't gunna like this."

Sarah patted Mattock on the shoulder and left with Howard, heading back into the alleyway.

Outside the station house there was a strange sound, like air escaping from a tyre.

Howard stopped and looked around. "What *is* that?"

Sarah eyes went wide. "I don—"

The third floor of the station house exploded. The wooden boards flew from the windows as flames burst through the openings. Bricks and stones rained on Sarah and Howard. A fist-sized piece of debris struck her shoulder, but she gritted her teeth and ignored it. Everything they needed was going up in flames.

Howard hit the deck and took cover. Sarah marched towards the burning building. Howard shouted at her to get back, but she couldn't be stopped. Burning rubble continued to rain on her, but all she could think about was the fact that every clue to finding Hesbani was inside the station house, on the third floor.

Sarah decided. She sprinted towards the building and burst through its front door. Clouds of smoke billowed at her—reminding her of the infirmary and Bradley's body—but she covered her mouth with the sleeve of her workman's jacket and made a beeline for the staircase.

Every step she took became more difficult, but she wouldn't let it stop her. She reached the next set of steps and felt heat from above. Fires raged everywhere, roaring as they consumed the rotten wood and super-heated the stonework.

The right side of Sarah's face started to sweat. The left side was incapable.

Howard's voice echoed from below, pleading for her to get out, but she couldn't go back until she knew there was nothing salvageable.

Sarah forced herself up the steps, battling the heat and smoke. She thought she might collapse a few times, but she willed herself to continue onwards.

The entire third floor was aflame. Embers fell from the ceiling timbers and filled the air like firebugs. Sarah flinched as a burning splinter sizzled on her neck. The desks and corkboards were up ahead, most of them consumed by flames, but one desk was only smouldering. She raced towards it.

Something hit Sarah on her back, knocking her onto her belly. She wheezed as a chunk of masonry pinned her to the floor; she choked as she tried to grab a breath, clawing at the floor. Her arms and legs tingled, and it took a concerted effort to move them.

Sarah rolled out from underneath the masonry, but could not get to her feet. She felt like she was swimming, and any attempt to get up only made her sink lower, so she crawled instead of walking, dragging herself towards the smouldering desk, trying to get there before it ignited.

She made it to the desk, now standing up was her next challenge. The flames licked at the legs of the table, so she couldn't use it for support. Her head flopped on her shoulders, and her hands clawed the air, but her eyes were alert and she spotted something lying beneath the table. There was a sheet of paper on the floor, blown free of the corkboard by the explosion. She snatched at it and shoved the paper into her trouser pocket, grinning at her victory.

But that was all she had. She was done.

Sarah lay like a rock, unable to move as the flames closed

in around her, consuming all in their path. She tried to cry out but could only manage a weak cough.

"Sarah!"

She couldn't see Howard, but his voice was coming from the stairs.

"Sarah, hold on."

Sarah waited, listening to the crackling of the flames. Then she felt herself hoisted upwards and dragged backwards through the smoke. She thought she might die, and if she did, she just hoped that the piece of paper in her pocket was useful.

AFGHANISTAN, 2008

As soon as Camp Bastion's patrol found Sarah, they rushed her back to base. There, a pair of Army surgeons rehydrated her and stitched up the festering wound in her thigh, but they couldn't do anything about her facial wounds. When she came around, they told her she'd been out for twenty-four hours. When she asked about her baby, they told her there was no baby, and nor would there ever be. She had miscarried during surgery and her uterus was shot. She hadn't cried upon hearing that, even though she felt more wretched than at any other point in her life.

At 0600 hours, Major Burke had come by to see her. He told her he was sorry for the loss of her child, and if she'd told him she was pregnant, he never would've sent her out. Sarah said it was okay and that it had been her decision not to tell him.

Then Major Burke had got down to business. "Sergeant Miller?"

"Dead."

"Private Owen?"

"Dead."

"Privates Murs, Styles, and McElderry?"

"Dead, dead, dead."

"Corporal Hamish Barnes?"

Sarah swallowed a lump in her throat. She couldn't look her CO in the eye when she spoke again. "Dead."

Burke sighed. "Christ, what a cluster fuck. We've blanketed the area in troops, but the village is abandoned. Seems like the Taliban had a stranglehold on the place, and we didn't even know it. We'll find these men, don't you worry, Captain."

But Sarah knew they wouldn't. Al-Sharir had eluded the West long enough to know what he was doing. He wouldn't be caught sleeping, and his right-hand man, Hesbani, was a rabid dog born for war. He would never be captured alive, and killing him would just make him the martyr he dreamed of being.

She needed to talk to Thomas. He needed to know about their baby. He needed to know how sorry she was. "I need to speak to my husband. Please, Major. He's at Camp Leatherneck. I need to see him."

Major Burke's face fell. He knew Thomas well, had even attended their wedding. He looked at Sarah now as if she'd asked for something he couldn't make sense of. "Sarah, I'm sorry. I tried to reach Thomas as soon as you came in. American Command told me he was carrying out a spec op in the area, leading a team of local insurgents in an unmarked minibus."

"Okay, when will the op be over?"

"That's the thing," Burke said. "One of our Apache patrols came across a bus in that area this morning. After what happened to your squad, we mistook it for hostile."

Sarah wanted to throw up. "I-Is Thomas okay?"

"No. The Apache fired on the bus. There were no

survivors. The bus was unmarked. We didn't know. I gave the order myself. I'm sorry."

Sarah closed her eyes. One week ago she was leaving the Army to start a family in sunny Florida with a man she adored. Now she had nothing.

Burke stood at the foot of her bed, looking at her with concern. "Sarah, do you understand what I've just told you?"

"Yes, I understand, sir. Now please get out of my fucking sight."

Sarah was discharged from the Army a week later.

22

THE PHANTOM MENACE

Firemen gave Sarah oxygen, and after several shaky hours, she finally got her breath back. The Fire Service dealt with the inferno before it spread outside the building and they were now trying to make the burnt-out building safe again.

Mattock dealt with the police while Howard stood beside Sarah in silence. The nearby rail station had been closed, and gawping spectators surrounded the area like ants around a biscuit. Another bomb had gone off in a small town, and the public's fear was tangible. British towns were going up like fireworks, and nobody knew where the devastation would hit next.

Sarah was still dealing with the fact that Hamish was alive —and working with Hesbani.

"You could have died going in there," Howard chided her. "What were you thinking?"

"If we don't catch Hesbani, there'll be more attacks. Maybe you should have been quicker following me in."

"We'll get him, Sarah, and we'll do it without you having to kill yourself. You're no good to us if you're dead."

"What the hell do you know about anything?" she snarled. "Hesbani ruined my life a long time ago, and now he's ruining hundreds more. The guy lives for this; he's a monster. If you don't have the stomach to get the job done, maybe you should go home."

"I'm just saying be careful. There's a difference between risk and stupidity."

"Did they teach you that when you were a university lecturer? This isn't a goddamn classroom, Howard. Theory goes out the window on the battlefield. You do what needs to be done, or you lose. I won't lose again, I can't."

"Well, guess what?" Howard said. "You just did lose. Hesbani got away. The lone wolf routine isn't working for you, Sarah. As for my time in the classroom, I used to think that predicting and preventing a terrorist's actions was better than dealing with the aftermath, when people are already dead. But, after one of my colleagues was arrested for poisoning a tea urn at a Christian fundraiser, I realised that you can't predict terrorism. It can't be studied or formulated. After thousands of years of human history, we still don't understand evil. My uncle was at that Christian fundraiser, and he *really* loved to drink tea." He swallowed. "Stop convincing yourself that being a bitch is okay just because you've lost something. You're not the only one who's suffered at the hands of evil. You're not special."

Sarah blinked and looked at her shoes.

Howard was still fuming, but after a minute he chuckled. "You know, the reason I brought you to MCU was because I thought we had something in common, but now I know that we don't. I do this because I want to save innocent lives, but you're doing this because you want to kill bad guys—and if you can't do that, you're happy to kill *yourself*. It's not courage, acting the way you do, it's cowardice. Face yourself in the mirror and decide you want to be human again. Do that and you'll have my respect. Until then, you're just a bitch."

Howard marched off before Sarah could respond. Even if he'd given her time, she wasn't sure she could've said anything. After everything that had happened, Sarah's head was a mess. She felt responsible for Bradley's death, but was angry that she'd ever been brought into this goddamn situation. Howard had asked for her help and she'd given it, but instead of gratitude she got anger from him.

Was everything really her fault?

She was scared. Scared of trusting, scared of finding out that she made it out of Afghanistan alive, while everyone around her had not. If she allowed herself a life again, would guilt overwhelm her? Would the faces of Miller, Thomas, and her baby haunt her? Or would they come back from the dead like Hamish?

Even if she wanted to let go of the past, what future could she even hope to have? She was a damaged freak.

Like a wild animal, Sarah let out a yell, screamed, kicked, and thrashed. She wanted to explode, to claw out her own eyes so that she wouldn't have to look at anyone ever again, but all she could do was flop to the floor in defeat as a flood of tears erupted from her.

"Bloody hell, girl. If your old man could see you now," said Mattock, approaching her.

Sarah glared at him. "He'd laugh at me, then walk away in shame, right? Don't you think I fucking know that? You can tell Daddy all about this at your next poker night. Have a laugh on me."

Mattock chuckled. "I wouldn't tell that miserable sod a damn thing. You're right, he would leave his daughter lying on the ground in tears, because that's the kind of man he is. No wonder you've got so many issues, luv. My old man was a bus driver, lovely man. Would have given his right arm for me if I needed it. Your old man is a cold-hearted bastard, you don't need to tell me."

Sarah choked on a sob. "I thought all the SAS loved my father. He's a hero."

"You're damn right he's a hero. Don't mean he's not a total arsehole, though. There're many things I miss about the forces, but Major Stone ain't one of 'em."

Sarah laughed, so unexpectedly that she ended up drooling. She wiped the spittle away with the back of her hand and laughed again. "That makes two of us," she said. "He could never forgive me for not having a cock between my legs."

Mattock offered Sarah his hand. "Believe me, any decent father would be proud to have a daughter like you."

Sarah didn't take Mattock's hand as she was too overwhelmed.

Mattock shifted. "Bloody hell, girl, will you get your arse up? I'm a trained killer, not a bleedin' nanny." He grabbed her under the arms and yanked her to her feet. "Man up, soldier. There're still arses to be kicked, and from what I can see, you still have both legs. Stop yer bawling."

Sarah nodded and wiped her eyes. "Okay, I'm done being a girl for today, and I'm also done losing. I think we're overdue for a big fucking win."

"Amen to that, Captain."

Sarah smiled at Mattock. "My friends call me Sarah."

"Sarah it is, then."

23

DADDY'S GIRL

Mattock talked with the police again while Sarah re-joined Howard. He looked like he was ready for a fight again as she approached him, but Sarah raised her hands to show she was coming in peace. "You were right," she said. "I might have a slight attitude problem."

"A *slight* problem?"

"Okay, fine, I'm a bitch, but I'm ready to play nice now. I know you've got my back. I've got yours too."

Howard smiled. "I know you do."

"We have nothing, Howard. Hesbani has planned more attacks, and we have no leads."

"Yes we do." He pulled a wedge of papers from his jacket pocket. "I held onto these after you gave them to me. It's the files on the suicide bombers."

Sarah grabbed Howard and kissed him hard on the mouth. "You beauty," she said. "We need to get these sent out right now."

Howard's cheeks reddened. "Already done it. I photographed the documents and sent them to Palu. He and Bennett are sending the info to every agency in the country.

Prime Minister Breslow herself has commended the MCU for its efforts. Whoever these disillusioned maniacs are, they'll be swept up within the hour."

Sarah was so relieved that they'd finally done some good. No matter what Hesbani did from here, they had foiled at least part of his plan. If they could capture some of the suicide bombers alive, they would have suspects to interview, information to gather.

"We'll get Hesbani," Howard told her. "Once we have his people, it's only a matter of time."

Sarah nodded. "I just hope we find him fast. He'll be desperate now—more dangerous than ever."

"And he still has people with him. We have no idea who the man in the balaclava was, or the woman in the van."

Sarah considered telling him about Hamish, but didn't quite know how to explain it. How could she tell Howard that she had let one of her men die in Afghanistan, but he was back from the grave?

Howard glanced at his sleeve and wiped off a layer of soot. Then he tugged at his cuffs and straightened up his workman's jacket. "Pity Hesbani's hideout went up in flames. It might have shed light on who his accomplices were. We still don't know if Al-Sharir is behind this."

Sarah's eyes went wide. "Balls, I forgot!"

Howard looked confused. "Huh?"

She pulled out the piece of paper she'd grabbed inside the burning building right before Howard had dragged her out. When she finished reading it, she looked up at Howard and swallowed. "This isn't good."

"What is it?"

Sarah handed him the piece of paper. "It's Hesbani's script for the final videotape."

Howard read it, his expression growing grim. "We have to get back to MCU. We can't let this happen."

Sarah raised her eyebrows. "No shit."

They left Mattock with the police and headed for the car. It had gotten late, the sun disappearing. Sarah put her foot down as she reached the M5 motorway heading south towards London. If Hesbani's plan was still active, London was where they needed to be. Within half an hour, they met up with Palu and Dr Bennett in the Earthworm's conference room.

Howard scanned Hesbani's script with his mob-sat and brought it up on the television screen.

People of Britain. Today your empire burns. Your capital city has crumbled, and your figurehead is dead. Such is the will of Allah. Shab Bekhier has carried out its mission as promised. You might try to stop us, you might try to kill us, but what we have done today will serve as a stark warning to future generations. My name is Al Al-Sharir, and all I have done, I have done for the glory of Allah.

"Why is Hesbani still claiming to be Al-Sharir?" Bennett asked. "Unless we're assuming that Al-Sharir might still be involved."

Sarah thought about Hamish, and how Al-Sharir had ordered Hesbani to slit his throat in the middle of the desert. "I don't know," she admitted. "Perhaps everything I thought about Al-Sharir is wrong. I thought he lived by a certain set of rules, a moral compass. Now, I'm not so sure."

Howard tapped his fingertips on the desk. "Have we brought in any of the documented suicide bombers yet?"

Palu answered. "Scotland Yard is carrying out a raid as we speak. As soon as they have them in custody, they know that finding Hesbani's whereabouts is top priority."

"We need to warn them that Hesbani's planning to take out Prime Minister Breslow," Bennett said.

"Are we sure about that?" asked Howard.

Bennett shrugged. "*Your figurehead is dead.* Who else could it be?"

"I suppose you're right," agreed Howard, "but how? The Prime Minister is the most protected woman in the country."

Bennett shook her head. "I disagree. In America there's a small army protecting our President, but your Prime Minister is virtually defenceless. There is no Secret Service to take a bullet for Breslow, or armed convoys taking her from one place to the next. Your Prime Minister is a soft target."

"She's right," Sarah said. "We don't plan for assassination attempts like other nations. With our gun ban and political system, the ramifications of executing a Prime Minister aren't worth the risk. The party in power would just put someone else in charge, and all the current policies would continue. The only reason to kill our Prime Minister is to make a statement. This whole thing has been about an eye-for-an-eye. We helped take out Saddam, Bin Laden, Gaddafi... now Hesbani wants to take out one of ours."

Palu stood. "I'll put through a call to Breslow. We have a prerogative to warn her."

Sarah leaned back and tried to think like Hesbani. Killing Breslow would be prime time news all over the world, but somehow it didn't quite fit. Breslow had only been in power for two years and had been behind a concerted effort to pull troops out of the Middle East. Her recent tax hikes and cutbacks on education had made her an unpopular leader, unlikely to get a second term. Killing her wouldn't crush the people of Great Britain. It wasn't grand enough. Hesbani wanted to be immortalised, but killing Breslow wouldn't gain him the everlasting notoriety that Bin Laden had achieved on 9/11.

Howard's mob-sat rang, and by the end of the call, he looked relieved. "Mandy's okay," he said. "His surgery was a success, and he's awake. Mattock is on his way to check on him right now."

"Good. Mandy promised to start a band with me, so he'd better be okay."

Howard smirked.

The sudden good news made Sarah think of things less fortunate. "What have we done with Bradley?"

"He's comfortable," Bennett said. "I wrapped him in blankets and laid him inside his dorm until we can have his body sent to his family."

"He had a room here?"

Bennett nodded. "There are dorm rooms in the rear of the head section. I can take you to him if you'd like."

Sarah nodded.

Dr Bennett took Sarah on the five minute walk to the dorms. "I'll leave you alone," she said when they reached Bradley's room.

"No. I'd like you to stay."

Bennett cleared her throat. "I... er... okay."

Bradley's body was wrapped in a bundle of white sheets on a small cot bed, a bible placed on top of his chest. "You're a Christian?" asked Sarah.

"Not really, but it seemed like the right thing to do. I don't know whether or not he believed. Seems like he was only around for a short while."

Sarah looked around the room, finding it cluttered. Bradley had tried to make it a home. A large black and white print of Trafalgar Square hung on one wall. On the other side of the room, an image of the royal crown hung above the inscription, *Keep Calm and Carry On.*

"What did you know about him?" Sarah asked.

Bennett shrugged. "He was a sweet boy, and smart. Loved his country, loved his queen, just wanted to do some good. I'm ashamed to say I underestimated how brave he was. In the end, he proved he was more than just a sweet boy."

"He loved the Queen?" Sarah found that odd.

"He loved everything about this country. Tell you the truth, I was never that happy about being posted here, but Bradley's enthusiasm was infectious. Brits can be rude and vulgar, and your roads make no sense at all, but deep down, y'all are about the most accommodating people on the planet. This country tries to please everybody all the time, and it probably comes about as close as any country could. America always prides itself on being free, but I've never been anywhere that's as free as Britain. You can be poor, sick, uneducated, or even from an enemy nation, and this country will look after you. That's why I'm happy to be here. I think this country is a place worth fighting for."

Sarah nodded. "Somehow I lost sight of that."

"You weren't fighting for your nation before, Sarah, you were fighting for your government. It's not the same. MCU is fighting the good fight, for no other agenda than saving lives. We don't care about oil, political favours, or international sanctions. The only thing we care about is stopping the bad guys. I think that's what you care about too. Perhaps it's the only thing left you care about."

Sarah looked at the doctor, and for the first time admired her. "Let me guess, you threw in a couple of psychology courses when you studied for your medical degree."

Bennett smiled. "Most doctors do. How else are we supposed to screw with y'alls heads?"

Sarah chuckled. "Thanks for not being the bitch I thought you were, Dr Bennett."

"Likewise."

Sarah heaved a sigh. "I need to say goodbye to Bradley, now."

Jessica nodded and left the room. Sarah knelt beside Bradley. "Hey kid, it's Sarah. I wanted to let you know that you were right. The problem wasn't with how other people saw me, it was about how I saw myself. If I hadn't met you, I might never have learned that lesson. I'm sorry I never got to be nicer to you. It's my fault you're dead, but I promise I will get Hesbani and make him pay. God save the Queen, Bradley."

24

INDEPENDENT WOMAN

"I informed Breslow," Palu told them. "She was dismissive. The Prime Minister is to remain in Downing Street until the current crisis is averted. People have rioted overnight in Birmingham and Bradford, with more trouble expected. She'll be holding conferences all day, so there won't be opportunity to take her out. She was scheduled to attend the VE Day river parade, but she's cancelled."

"She should have cancelled the whole parade," Sarah said. "We're in the midst of a terrorist campaign, and people are packing their sandwiches to go stand by the river."

Howard was frowning. "Hesbani has this all wrong. He'd know that Prime Minister would remain at Downing Street after all these attacks. Why would he not assassinate her first, then explode the suicide bombs?"

"Something about this doesn't add up," agreed Sarah. "I don't buy Breslow as a big enough target for Hesbani. He wants to become a hero to the terrorist community. Breslow isn't important enough."

"I dare say I agree," Bennett said. "No disrespect, but your

Prime Minister is a fairly benign figure in world events. Assassinating Sir Ian McKellen would hurt the country more."

Howard winced. "Nobody wants to see Gandalf die."

"So what are we thinking, then?" Palu asked. "Who's a bigger target than the Prime Minister? Who's the 'figurehead' Hesbani plans to assassinate?"

"The Queen," Sarah said, knowing it to be true. Bradley's unashamed love for the royal family was indicative of a large portion of the country. The Queen was the very embodiment of British pride, a symbol of the British Empire. "Hesbani wants to punish us for our imperialistic past. What person represents the British Empire more than the Queen?"

"There's no way of knowing for certain," Howard said, "but I buy it. The Queen would be the jewel in a terrorist's crown, excuse the pun."

"How could Hesbani hope to assassinate the Queen?" Bennett said. "She's hardly ever in public."

"Except for today," Howard said. "It's May eighth, VE Day. The Queen is scheduled to travel via barge down the Thames. She'll be awarding veteran medals on the stretch of river in front of Westminster at the end of the River Parade."

Sarah shook her head. "How the hell can we be having a parade when half-a-dozen villages have been bombed?"

"That's exactly why," Palu said. "The Queen has already spoken out against the terrorists, clarifying that her plans will not be altered by fear or demand. Today is about remembering the men and woman who fight for our freedom. It would be a great disservice to cancel because of monsters like Hesbani."

"I can see why Bradley loved the old dear," Sarah commented. "She's got balls."

"We should warn Her Majesty," Bennett said.

Sarah shook her head. "If we do that, Hesbani might

disappear. Our best chance of getting him is out in the open. He doesn't know what we found at the station house. As long as he remains in the dark, we have the upper hand."

Bennett folded her arms. "It's unethical not to warn her."

"So is letting Hesbani escape."

Palu motioned for silence. "We'll hold off on warning the royal household for now, but we don't know what other threats Hesbani might be planning. We need to take him alive and before any more bombs go off. The speech mentions that our capital is in ruins. I believe there are more targets we don't yet know about."

Howard bashed his fist on the desk. "Christ! Where does this end?"

"I think he'll be focused on hitting Westminster," Sarah said. "Hesbani will want something iconic. What would be a more lasting image than the Houses of Parliament burning?"

Palu nodded. "We need to get bodies on the ground. Howard and Sarah, get to Westminster and find Hesbani. Dr Bennett and I will coordinate from here. The Scotland Yard swoop is in progress as we speak. Soon as I hear anything, I'll let you know what we have."

Sarah nodded. "What about Mattock's team? We need everyone we can get."

"Agreed. As soon as Mandy is here, I'll send Mattock to assist you. Get yourselves armed; I want you on the road in ten."

"Good work, partner," Howard told Sarah as they left the conference room.

"We're not partners yet."

Howard frowned.

She patted him on the back. "I still need to earn that honour."

Howard took her to the armoury again where she replaced

her stolen SIG with another. They both strapped on Kevlar vests beneath their clothes and then left.

Sarah knew her way around the Earthworm well enough by now that she made it out into the derelict farm only a few minutes later. The MCU was starting to feel like home.

She and Howard started the remaining Jag and got going. By the time they reached the highway, the lunchtime rush had started. Despite all the devastation, people still had to earn a living.

Once upon a time, the people of Britain would have banded together in a crisis, lining the streets in solidarity. Nowadays, people acted like nothing had happened. They lived life as individuals, where once they had been a community. Sarah wondered if the country would ever get back to those days of unified spirit.

The lunchtime rush hour resulted in the drive being more than an hour. By the time they parked on Great College Street—opposite Big Ben—it was 1.30PM. The Queen was due to appear at 3PM.

Howard rummaged in the boot of the Jag for his jacket while Sarah surveyed the area. Westminster seemed ancient in the soft sunlight. The sharp spikes of the Parliament buildings caught the light and sparkled like a castle out of Camelot. The nearby river added to the fantasy. What ruined it was the endless lines of beeping traffic and photo-snapping tourists. People already lined the banks of the Thames, investing hours of their time to get a decent spot for the short-lived festivities. Sarah hoped they didn't end up getting a show they weren't expecting. If the Queen was shot, the whole world would see it, live. Even now, there were news helicopters hovering. Their cameras wouldn't miss a thing. It was the grandest place in the city, making it the grandest place to assassinate a monarch.

"Where do we start?" Howard asked, closing the boot. He

handed her a small radio which she attached to the lapel of her jacket.

"The officers killed in front of Scotland Yard were hit by a sniper, right? My guess would be that Hesbani is planning to hit Her Majesty as she comes down the river."

Nearby, a gentleman smoking a cigarette gave her an astonished glance. He'd obviously heard her.

"Hey," Sarah shouted at the guy. "Go smoke that somewhere else before I stub it out in your eye."

The man hurried away.

Howard frowned. "I thought you were going to go with a different attitude."

"I am. Did you hear me use any bad language?"

Howard smirked. "Well done."

"Thank you. Now, if I were a sniper, where would I perch?"

Howard looked up at Big Ben. "How 'bout up there?"

Sarah considered the bell tower behind the giant clock and knew it looked right out over the Thames. If for nothing else, it would be a good place for Sarah and Howard to survey the area.

"Okay, make a call or something. Get us inside."

Howard called Palu, who got them clearance right away. There was a security guard at the front entrance who was expecting them, and they were shown inside.

"How easy is it to access Big Ben," Sarah glanced at the guard's name badge, "David?"

"Technically, Big Ben is the name of the bell, sweetheart. The tower itself is called the Elizabeth Tower. To answer your question, though, there are sporadic tours, usually arranged by local MPs trying to impress their constituents, but during special occasions the tower is off-limits. Bomb threats are the greatest concern, especially on days like today. What are you, MI5, Special Branch? I was going to apply to join the Met, but got myself a dodgy knee. So what are you looking for? You can tell me, I've signed all the confidentiality forms."

"What about snipers?" asked Howard, ignoring David's babble.

David shrugged. His shoulders were wide but his belly was fat. It didn't look like the guy had ever made the trip to the top of the tower himself. "It's a good spot, I guess, but this place is never empty. I think a sniper probably wants to be hidden, don't he, so this wouldn't be a good place."

Sarah was disappointed. Hesbani would not be so predictable. She wondered if he was the sniper, or was it Hamish, or the woman in the burka? She didn't remember Hamish having any particular skill with a rifle, and Hesbani's fondness for knives made her pretty sure he wouldn't be found behind a sniper's scope. That left the women in the burka. Who the hell was she?

"Can we go to the bell tower?" Sarah asked the guard.

David nodded and led them to the top. "I'll be back at the entrance," he said. "You need anything just holler."

From inside the tower, Sarah could see the sunshine gleaming off the river bathing the city in an orange halo. From up so high, the city noise disappeared. It was beautiful.

"Don't suppose you can see anything?" Howard asked.

Sarah shook her head. "It's like an ant farm down there. We'll never spot anything from up here without a telescope."

"Try these." Howard handed her a small, sleek set of binoculars.

"Where did you get these?"

"Out of the boot. You didn't think I'd come on a surveillance mission with nothing to *survey* with, did you?"

Sarah snatched the binoculars. "Knew you would come in handy someday."

"Hey, you're the one who has to keep being rescued."

"Those days are over," said Sarah, "and as I remember it, you've been a damsel in distress yourself since we met, too."

"Maybe our odds would be better if we stuck together."

Sarah frowned. Howard stood like a boy asking a girl out on a first date. "If you're asking me to be your partner," she said, "I'm afraid I already promised myself to one of Dr Bennett's cats."

Howard punched the air. "Those damned cats, always in on my action."

Sarah giggled and then remembered why they were there. She looked through the binoculars, and London came back to life. The ants had become people and cars again.

"There are people everywhere," she said. "I don't even know what to look for."

"The parade is set to begin soon," Howard said. "We need to look out for anybody acting outside of expected parameters. Commuters should be moving, and tourists should be spectating and taking pictures. Is there anybody doing something different?"

Sarah scanned below. Just as Howard had predicted, there were several lines of suited business people trying to get where they're going as quickly as possible. Their main obstacles were the dawdling groups of tourists taking photographs, or standing and pointing. It was like watching a river flowing around boulders.

Various boats, mostly small outboard vessels, lined the width of the Thames, each of them emblazoned with Union Jacks and other patriotic symbols. There were also Nepalese, Cypriote, and several other national emblems for those who had aided Britain during the Second World War.

To Sarah's left was the *London Eye*. The city's giant Ferris Wheel could make a good spot for a sniper, but while it was moving, it would require a lot of on-the-fly adjustments. It couldn't be ruled out as a possible location, but it wasn't ideal. There were many other buildings on the opposite side of the river, but none were particularly tall. They would also be extremely busy during a working day which made the likelihood of discovery high.

Where would I want to be if I was going to set up a rifle? Somewhere high with a nice long approach, target coming towards me, not across me. I would want to be invisible.

Sarah scanned with the binoculars but kept coming up empty. The best place to snipe a boat coming down the river was from atop Westminster Bridge, but the road was flat and low. There were no elevations or interior spaces in which to hide like there was in Tower Bridge. Sarah hated to admit it, but she didn't think they would find the sniper at this section of the Thames.

Howard was silent behind her, obviously sensing her frustration. If she didn't find a clue, they'd be forced to warn the queen's security. The parade would be cancelled, and even more panic would descend upon the country. And Hesbani would disappear into the woodwork.

Sarah took one last look, wishing with all her damaged soul to find something. She checked out the ferry boats departing from Westminster Pier, the buses crossing the bridge, the carriages on the London Eye, and the office buildings on the opposite bank. She was just about to give up when she spotted something on the other side of the river. "Howard, what's that building across the river with the big green tower?"

"Er... County Hall. There's a *Sea Life* centre there and some restaurants."

Sarah nodded and kept the binoculars to her eyes. "Well, right now there's a black van with a rear spoiler broken down at the side of the road."

Howard blanched. "You're kidding. The same one we saw at the station house in Redditch?"

Sarah studied the van and was certain. Its hazard lights were blinking, and one of its tyres was flat. "Come on," she said to Howard. "We've got the bastards."

They raced down Elizabeth Tower and bumped into the guard, David, at the bottom.

"Everything good?" he asked.

"Ask me in ten minutes," Sarah told him. "If it looks like I just kicked the shit out of someone, then yes, everything is absolutely dandy."

25

FAMILY

Sarah and Howard raced for the car. Sarah's heart was thumping. Every second it took to reach the van was a second Hesbani could be getting away. When they reached the Jag, Sarah threw herself into the driver's seat, ignoring the agony of her multiple wounds, and reversed before Howard even got fully in the car.

Crossing over Westminster Bridge, Sarah had to fight the urge to batter the horn. Traffic crawled between pedestrian-covered pavements, but the last thing she could afford was to alert Hesbani they were coming. There was also a chance she was racing headlong into danger, but there was no time to worry about that now.

Howard got on the radio. "Palu, we have a possible target sighting. North bank, outside County Hall. Black transit van with rear, roof-mounted spoiler. Alert authorities. Back-up needed."

"Roger that," Palu came back. "Will alert local authorities. Mattock en route to provide back-up."

"Tell him to hurry his arse up," she said. "I could really use him about now."

"Roger that. Engage target if necessary, but be careful. You don't know what to expect."

"Don't worry," Sarah said. "The only people dying today are terrorists."

The radio clicked off, and Sarah put her foot down as the traffic opened ahead. She glanced at Howard beside her. "You ready, partner?"

"Hell yes. Time to kick Hesbani's arse."

She laughed. "You sound like me."

"Not necessarily a bad thing."

"Don't get soppy on me."

"Wouldn't dream of it, Captain."

"It's Sarah. Now, let's do this." They reached the end of the bridge and raced into oncoming traffic, crossing the lanes and heading for the parked-up van on the other side. There was a cacophony of blaring horns and swerving tyres, but it was too late for Hesbani to get an early warning. The Jag skidded to a stop right in front of the van.

"Police," Sarah shouted, leaping out of the car. "Or something like that." She pulled out her SIG, and nearby pedestrians scattered. Mobile phones appeared out of pockets and went up in the air. Some dialled 999 while others captured video footage.

Howard and Sarah each approached opposite sides of the van. Sarah took the passenger side with the sliding door. The windows were blacked out, but Sarah could see that there was nobody in the front seat. "I'm opening the side door," she shouted to Howard. "I'm going after three."

"Roger that."

"One…" Sarah threw the door open, trying to catch any occupants unaware. The plan didn't work as she was the one taken by surprise. Hamish leapt out of the van, smashing his meaty forehead into Sarah's face.

Sarah staggered backwards as she felt her nose break. The blood came thick and fast, but she was determined. She blinked away the tears and wiped away the blood with the back of her sleeve. Then she growled.

Hamish took off in a fast limp, the wound where she'd shot him wrapped in a thick white bandage. As he ran, he fired wildly behind him, causing chaos in the streets.

Sarah was about to go after Hamish, ready to chase him to the ends of the earth, but Howard stood in her way. He pointed to the van's interior, his face stark white.

Sarah glanced quickly, then choked. "Holy shit balls! Is that what I think it is?"

The van's rear compartment was chock-full of plastic explosives. Bricks of the stuff had been piled on top of a wooden pallet. At either end of the pallet were dozens of glass containers filled with amber liquid. Whatever it was, there were enough explosives inside the van to wipe Westminster off the map.

Sarah looked towards the bridge. Hamish was getting away. "There's nothing I can do here," she told Howard. "Call this in. I'm going after Hamish."

Howard shook his head, confused. "Who?"

Sarah realised she hadn't yet explained about Hamish, but there was no time to get into it now. "Just call it in," she said, and then sprinted towards the bridge. Already, she was losing sight of Hamish, but she would not let him get away. Not this time.

Sarah sprinted, reaching a speed she'd not managed since her days in the army—before her thigh had been torn up by IED shrapnel. It felt good to have her muscles moving in sync again; her entire body focused towards the single goal of momentum. It was a rebirth. The tiredness and pain of the last few days had ebbed away, and she felt strong and powerful, fully awake for the first time in years.

Sarah caught sight of Hamish and gained on him. He wasn't in the shape he had been six years ago, and the wound in his leg was slowing him down. Several times, he glanced over his shoulder at her and saw she was closing the distance between them. He was halfway across the bridge when he realised he wasn't going to get away. He stopped and pointed his gun at her. It was the SIG he had taken from Sarah.

"Stop right there, Captain," he yelled at her. "Not another wee step, yer hear me?"

Sarah slowed right down, but still strolled towards him. She had her own weapon out now, but kept it hanging by her thigh. "You're done Hamish. We know all about Hesbani's plan. We've got your van full of explosives, and we'll find your stashed rifle. It was a stupid plan, you were never a marksman."

Hamish grinned. "Aye, you're right there. I never was much cop with a rifle, was I? I only joined the Army to avoid the doll queues. Still, I was a loyal soldier all the way, straight as an arrow, for all the good it did me."

Sarah wasn't about to get dragged into the past, not when she was finally ready to let it go. "You're going to have much more to worry about than the unemployment line when this is all over, Corporal. What the hell were you thinking, working with Hesbani? He slit your throat, Hamish. I watched him do it."

"Aye, he did, but it wasn't him what killed me; it was you, remember? You made the choice." He lifted his head to show a swollen scar across his throat that almost put Sarah's wounds to shame. It was a thick pink slug, slithering from ear to ear.

"I'm sorry," Sarah said, and meant it. "I made the wrong decision. I was afraid, and it made me selfish. It still doesn't explain all this though. Killing innocent people doesn't make anything better. It doesn't make anything right."

The sound of sirens came from both sides of the river. Police arrived in squad cars and blocked both ends of the bridge.

Sarah raised her SIG, pointing it right at Hamish's chest. "You're finished, Corporal. Stand down."

Hamish laughed. "A captain is supposed to protect his men. You chose your own well-being over mine. You turned your back on me and then guess what?"

"What?"

"The goddamn government refused to pay my daughter any money because I wasn't confirmed dead."

Sarah hadn't even known Hamish had a daughter. "I told them you were dead. I said I saw you die."

"Aye, I'm sure yer did. Didn't stop 'em welching on their obligation to look after my family, though. Fucking crooks."

"But you're not dead," said Sarah, reaffirming her grip on her gun. "So they didn't owe you anything anyway."

Hamish growled, hatred seething from his pores. "I was left for dead and abandoned by my bloody captain, not to mention being kept prisoner for a year. Believe me, that's as good as dead."

"So what changed? When did you go from prisoner to terrorist?"

"I'm not the terrorist, the UK government is the terrorist. I realised that when one of their bombs hit a school in the Afghani village I was being held in. Do you know what it's like to see children on fire? It changes you. After that day, I begged Hesbani to let me help him get revenge. Six months later, he finally trusted me enough to let me go back home, working for Shab Bekhier."

Sarah sighed, and her gun lowered. "Mistakes happen in war."

"I'll never accept that," Hamish spat. "Not if it means seeing more innocent children die."

"Your bombs have killed children in this country. You're a hypocrite."

Hamish sneered. "Our children aren't innocent. They're brats bred on consumption. Their sacrifice will help save the truly innocent."

"What happened to the man I served with?" Sarah asked. "You were never like this. You wanted to help the people of Afghanistan."

"He was left to die in the desert."

"What could I have done?"

Hamish swallowed and looked like he might combust with his hatred for her. "You could have done your job and protected your men. You could have saved me, but you chose yourself and that fucking baby inside of you."

Sarah swallowed. "You understand nothing, Hamish. You think I got away scot free? I died in that desert just the same as you did."

"We should never have been there. Don't you realize that? Look what they did to you. Did they treat you like a hero for all that you gave? Did they apologise for what happened to your face?"

Sarah thought about how she'd been discarded after her blow-up at Major Burke in her hospital bed. The Army liked to make out that an injured soldier only had themselves to blame. The report had said: 'Captain Stone breached protocol by assisting an unidentified civilian.' It went on to blame her for the death of her squad. The woman with the watermelons had ended Sarah's life, but it was her own government who put dirt on her coffin. "No, they didn't treat me like a hero," she admitted, "because I wasn't one."

"Then what are you doing, Captain? Why are you fighting for a country that doesn't give a wee shit about you?"

"I'm not doing it for my country; I'm doing it for twenty-nine dead children."

"Well, I suppose we have something in common then."

"I suppose we do." Sarah raised her SIG and let off a shot. She hit Hamish in the shoulder, knocking her original SIG from his hand and rocking him against the railings. As his sleeve rolled up, Sarah spotted a dagger tattoo on his wrist.

Hamish gritted his teeth and started to sag. He spat blood. "You don't even know what you're fighting for, Sarah."

"You're finished, Corporal. Stand down before I put you down."

Hamish grunted. "I may be finished, but Hesbani isn't. You really think I'm the shooter? I couldn't hit a barn door with a rocket launcher. You have the right plan, but the wrong player."

Sarah took a step forward, lowering her SIG. "Talk. Who's the shooter?"

Hamish just grinned.

Sarah fired off a shot into his knee. The sound of more gunfire brought armed police hurrying up each end of the bridge. They approached cautiously, shouting warnings to stand down.

Hamish slumped to the ground, clutching his knee and gritting his teeth as he continued refusing to give voice to the pain.

Sarah pointed the gun at his head. "I'll give you credit, you're a lot tougher than I remember."

"Conviction does that to a man. Do what you want. My conscience is clean. Is yours?"

Sarah pressed the gun against Hamish's forehead. "Might as well send you on your merry way then. Ready to see what's waiting for you on the other side? I'm pretty sure there won't be any virgins for you."

"If you kill me, the police will take you down. Whoever you're working with, you don't have the authority to kill people in the middle of a London street."

Sarah saw spiraling helicopters converged above Westminster Bridge and the police at either end. Hamish was right. If she fired one more shot, the police would shoot her.

The radio on Sarah's lapel squawked as Howard's voice came though. "Sarah, the bomb squad are on their way. The Met have called off the parade. The Queen is already onboard her royal barge, but she's being returned to HMS *Britannia* under heavy guard. She'll remain onboard there until the threat has passed. It's over, Sarah. Let the police take things from here."

Sarah turned the radio off. She removed the muzzle of her gun from Hamish's forehead and stepped back. "You've lost," she said. "The Queen is safe. They're taking her to safety right now."

Hamish spat blood on the pavement. "You think so? Far as I see it, Her Majesty is still out in the open. Doesn't sound like she's safe to me."

Sarah frowned. "Where is the sniper? Where is Hesbani?"

"You'll never get to him in time. Doesn't matter where the Queen is; he'll be able to get her."

The choppers overhead circled. Sarah knew now where to find Hesbani, but before she could ask more questions, Hamish leapt up on his good leg and shoved himself against the railing. At first, Sarah thought he was going to make a grab for her gun, but then he threw himself over the railing. By the time Sarah reacted, there was nothing below but frothing water where Hamish had landed.

With the situation defused, the police started up either end of the bridge. They pointed assault rifles at Sarah and shouted for her to drop her weapon and hit the ground. Sarah held onto her SIG for the time being though. It was the only thing keeping the police from rushing her. She opened up her radio so that MCU could hear her, but she also spoke loudly enough that the police heard her too. She didn't care who was listening just so long as somebody was. "There's still a terrorist threat. The Queen is in danger. I think the sniper is in a news chopper."

"DROP YOUR WEAPON!"

She carried on. "There is going to be an attempt on the Queen's life any minute."

"DROP YOUR WEAPON, OR WE WILL FIRE."

Sarah eased her grip on the SIG, but couldn't bring herself to drop it. As soon as she did that, the police would rush her and take her out of the game.

"THREE SECONDS. THREE..."

Sarah swallowed.

"TWO..."

A voice came over Sarah's radio. "Sarah, I hear you loud and clear, mate. Looks like you could do with a lift out of there, sharpish."

It was Mattock. Sarah gushed when she heard his calm cockney voice. "Mattock. Shit, I could really do with a way out of this."

"Roger that. I'm here to drag your arse out of the fire, luv."

Sarah glanced around the bridge. "Where are you?"

"Right behind you."

Sarah was blown sideways as the Griffin helicopter swooped beside the bridge. The police were taken by surprise too and leapt into cover behind the railings. Sarah shielded her hair to stop it blinding her.

"Stop pissing around and hop onboard," yelled Mattock. "Time's a wasting."

Sarah glanced at the police squads. They were already getting up and coming back towards her. She had to move now.

Screw it!

She hopped back to get a run up and then sprinted towards the railing. She leapt into the air, spiking her foot on top of the steel railing and launching herself off the bridge. For a moment, it felt like she was flying.

Voices of the police shouting at her faded away as she began to fall. The river blurred beneath her.

Mattock grabbed a hold of her in mid-air and dragged her onboard. She ended up on her face, ankles dangling out the door.

"You okay, Sarah?"

She flipped up onto her knees and nodded. "Just glad to see you."

"Where's Hesbani?"

"I don't know for sure, but I think he might be in a news chopper."

Mattock helped her to her feet. Nice quick exit after the deed is done. "No place I'd rather be as a sniper. The Queen is en route east to the HMS *Britannia*."

"Then that's where we head. Wait, who's piloting this thing?"

Mattock nodded to the cockpit. "Mandy. No one I'd rather have at the stick, even with a bullet wound in his chest."

Sarah climbed into the co-pilot's seat and looked across at Mandy. He was focused on jinking the helicopter left and right with unnatural skill. There was a bulge beneath his shirt where a heavy bandage no doubt covered his wound.

"You okay?" she asked him.

He turned to her, a blank expression on his face, and then said, "Just a flesh wound. Glad you're still with us, Captain."

As Sarah watched the deep lines of focus on the big pilot's face, along with the protective stares from Mattock in the back, Sarah couldn't help but feel like she was among family.

26

KICK OFF

Sarah joined Mattock at the rear of the helicopter where he was adjusting the sights on an AR-15. "I didn't bring anything bigger," he apologised, "but Mandy can loose a couple of Hellfires if need be."

Sarah hated hellfire missiles; they were too indiscriminate. "There are too many boats down there. There'll be casualties."

"What's the plan, then? How do we stop Hesbani if he's airborne?"

Sarah shrugged. "When the time comes, we'll do whatever we have to do, but we have to find him now, before it's too late."

The HMS *Britannia* floated ahead, not as large as its name implied. The Queen's barge sailed nearby, easy to identify from its lavish red and gold accoutrements.

"There's a dozen choppers up ahead," Mandy said. "How do we know which one we're looking for?"

"Can we hail them?" Sarah asked.

Mandy nodded and fiddled with the dashboard knobs. "Be advised, all aircraft in the vicinity of HMS *Britannia*, please identify. Possible terrorist threat, please be advised."

The radio squawked back with pilots from other helicopters. Some obliged and broke away while others were newshounds unwilling to lose sight of the Queen. By the time Mandy got off the radio, only three helicopters remained.

"Who do we have left?" Mattock said.

Sarah peered out the side hatch and tried to make out the decals on the other helicopters. "Never Stop News, BBC World, and… the third is too far away."

"Get us up close, Mandy," Mattock ordered.

The Griffin tilted forward and picked up speed. They passed the Never Stop News chopper first and Sarah tried to see who was inside—could just about make out the shape of a man in the pilot's seat. He waved to her as she passed. Seeing inside the BBC chopper was much easier: a crew of three inside, but none of them Hesbani.

"It has to be the last chopper."

"If they have a high-powered rifle," Mattock said with a hint of panic, "they can take a shot at the Queen any time."

Sarah watched the slow-moving barge with the royal regalia. Any sniper worth his salt would be setting up their shot right now.

"Unidentified civilian aircraft, this is HMS Britannia. You are not cleared for this airspace. Please leave the area immediately."

Sarah jumped into the co-pilot's seat and grabbed the intercom. "HMS *Britannia*, this is… *Agent* Stone of the MCU. We are in pursuit of a suspected terrorist. Please be advised: imminent threat to Her Majesty. Repeat: imminent threat to Her Majesty."

"Stand down, civilian aircraft. You are in restricted airspace. Leave the area or face hostile response."

"Do what you gotta do, dickhead. I'm not leaving until the threat has been dealt with." Sarah turned the intercom off and turned to Mattock. "Call Palu, see if he can buy us some time."

Mattock was already on his mob-sat. "On it."

When they got closer to the final helicopter, Sarah saw that it belonged to one of Rupert Murdoch's rags. Mandy edged up alongside it as Sarah prepared to fire her SIG. But there were only dumbfounded expressions to be found inside: three middle-aged men in turtle-necks. Sarah recognised one of them from the evening news.

"Shit, it's not them! It's not the right chopper."

As if to prove her point, there was an ear-piercing *ping* as something hit the Griffin's hull.

Ping!

"Some cheeky bugger's shooting at us," Mattock growled. "Mandy, take us up. It must be the Britannia."

"No," Mandy said, "we're being fired at from the rear." He pulled back on the yoke and Sarah and Mattock stumbled to the back of the cabin. The wind howled through the open side hatch as the helicopter spun around.

"They must be in the first chopper," Sarah shouted over the bellow of the engines. "Never Stop News. Get us close, Mandy."

Mandy didn't reply, but the helicopter zipped back and forth, making the Griffin a hard target for sniper fire.

Mattock grabbed hold of a seat and grimaced at her. "I'm gonna chuck my bloody guts up in a minute."

"Grow some balls," Sarah told him. "There's worse than this at Disney World."

"I never pegged you for a *Mouseketeer*," Mattock said, trying not to heave.

The cabin tilted, and Sarah swung from the nylon hand holds above her like a rag doll, her feet flailing in thin air.

Ping!

"Shit, we're in the line of fire again," Mattock said. "Mandy, get us out of their sights."

The chopper zipped sideways at 90-degrees. Sarah's legs swung around in a circle as she held on for dear life.

Snap!

Sarah hit the floor of the cabin and moaned in agony. The nylon hand hook was still wrapped around her wrist, but the rigging had come loose from its ceiling rivets.

Mandy righted the chopper and Mattock yanked Sarah to her feet. "You went a bit of a pisser there, luv."

Sarah shrugged free of him and strapped herself in beside Mandy up front. She turned to him and saw the glint in his eyes. "You're enjoying this, aren't you?"

Mandy stared back at her with his typical poker face, but this time she was sure there was a grin at the corners of his mouth

They hurtled forwards through the air, heading for the Never Stop News chopper. It was a game of chicken now, but they were playing against a suicide bomber. In a game of chicken, a suicide bomber always won.

Sarah was relieved when Mandy dove underneath the other chopper, just as they were about to collide. The Griffin swooped through the air in a long arc and came up behind its target. They gained on the other chopper, which also had its side door open.

Sarah knew they'd found their sniper.

Hanging out of the door with a long, scoped rifle was the woman in the burkha. Sarah narrowed her eyes and concentrated. Something about the woman was familiar. She was covered from head to toe with only her hands and eyes showing, but Sarah couldn't help but think she knew her.

Then she realised.

The woman in the burkha had the sniper rifle propped over her left wrist. She was using her wrist because her hand was missing.

Sarah's mouth dropped. "It can't be."

"What?" Mattock still looked like he might vomit.

"I know the shooter," Sarah said. "She was responsible for the death of my squad in Afghanistan."

"You mean the woman with the watermelons?"

"You know about that?"

"We all know about that. It's in your file." He placed a hand on her shoulder. "Think you owe that mad tart some payback, don't you?"

Sarah nodded. Mattock's hand on her shoulder felt nice. For the first time in a long time, somebody had her back. Instead of blaming her for her past mistakes, Mattock wanted to help her make them right again.

Sarah unclipped herself from the co-pilot seat and held her SIG up in front of her. One well-placed shot would put an end to a whole lot of emotional baggage.

The Never Stop News chopper was just ahead of the Griffin. Sarah leaned out of the side hatch and brought up her aim.

PING!

She flinched back inside. The bullet had hit the hull an inch from her skull. She leaned back out and tried to get a shot off again.

PING!

"Damn it," she said. "I won't be able to get a shot while she's zeroed in on us. She's too good."

Mattock went up to the side door and blindly fired his AR-15. It was more a show of support than anything else.

PING!

"Shit!" Mattock dropped the assault rifle out of the hatch and fell backwards into the cabin, clutching his bleeding hand. "Bugger it," he said. "That was my Monopoly-playing hand."

Sarah helped Mattock into a seat just as the cockpit window shattered, turning the interior of the helicopter into a wind tunnel. Mandy cursed from the pilot's seat and gained altitude.

PING!

The shot came from beneath them, hitting the underside of the hull. Mandy tilted the chopper sideways and headed away.

"We can't get near them," Mattock said. "We're going to end up in the Thames if we keep taking fire like this."

"As soon as she gets some distance from us, she's going to line up a shot on the Queen," Sarah said.

Mattock growled. "The old bird must be under cover by now. How is the shooter planning on getting a line on her?"

"I don't know," admitted Sarah, "but if I know Hesbani, he won't accept failure. The threat isn't over until he's stopped."

"Then what the hell do we do, luv?"

Sarah stood up and looked around the cabin before scrambling back into the cockpit. "Mandy, is it safe to get above the other chopper?"

Mandy nodded. "It'll keep us out of the line of sight, but they'll also be out of ours. We won't be able to do anything."

Sarah knew that. "I have an idea," she said. "Take us right above them. Then, when I give the word, bring us out ten feet on their right—tight as possible to their top. You understand?"

Mandy didn't question her, just nodded.

Sarah headed back into the cabin and knelt.

"What you doing?" Mattock asked her.

"Ever see Tarzan?"

Sarah picked up the nylon rigging and straightened it out. There was about twelve feet of it. She went to Mattock's seat and reached underneath him.

"Aye up, luv. I'm married."

Sarah rolled her eyes. "So am I." She looped the nylon rope around the fitting beneath Mattock's seat, yanking it tight. It'd only have to be strong enough to hold her for a second.

Mattock gave her the strangest look then. "You're not about to do what I think you are, are you?"

Sarah grinned. "I'd never try to understand the mind of a man, so who knows what you're thinking."

She wrapped the other end of the nylon rope around her waist and made sure it was secure. Then she stood in the open hatch and stared down at the whirling propeller blades of the other chopper. "Mandy," she shouted, "take us to the right, just like I said."

The chopper moved. The whirling blades beneath Sarah shifted away until there was an opening gap between the two helicopters. The one-handed woman was unaware that Sarah was hovering above her, which was why she was setting up to take her shot at the Queen. She was no longer holding the high-powered rifle she had been firing at the Griffin, but a Javelin Missile launcher. She was going to take out the entire barge.

Here goes nothing!" Sarah took a deep breath and jumped out the side of the helicopter. She immediately regretted it. She kicked at thin air, the wind rushing to meet her and lethal propellers whirling beneath. She fell within mere inches of the deadly blades and carried on falling.

The nylon rope caught and went taut. Sarah's body jolted, and she was thrown forwards. The rope hit the propellers and snapped in two. Suddenly, she was flying, held in place by nothing but gravity and momentum. Her swing threw her forward, right into the side hatch of the other chopper. She landed on top of the woman in the burka, and the Javelin launcher clattered against the floor.

Sarah kicked out a leg and booted it out of the cabin and into the Thames.

A fist hit Sarah's jaw and sent her rolling across the floor.

The woman in the burka was a wild animal, clawing and hissing, punching at Sarah's face with both her right fist and left stump. Sarah saw stars as she tried to find an opening into the fight.

Sarah grabbed the woman's headdress, using it as leverage. The burka came free, and Sarah was faced with the woman who had blown her friend, Sergeant Miller, to pieces.

The woman glared at Sarah, teeth bared like a wolf. Her eyes were a deep brown, and small scars criss-crossed the weathered skin of her nose and cheeks.

"Fucking 'ell," Sarah said. "You're uglier than I am." She whipped her SIG out of its holster and smashed the butt against the woman's nose, breaking it with ease. The woman sprawled away from Sarah, hitting the bench against the far side of the cabin. Sarah prepared to fire her SIG, but the sound of a gun cocking behind her head halted her.

Sarah turned to find Hesbani in the cockpit, aiming a gun at her face. "I believe you and my sister have met before. What a reunion this is. Aziza, are you okay?"

The woman clutched her broken nose but grunted in affirmation. Sarah kept her SIG aimed at the woman's head. "You have a lovely family, Hesbani. I didn't know inbreeding was so prevalent in Afghanistan."

"I have very little family," Hesbani replied. "Thanks to the immoral West."

Sarah rolled her eyes. "God, you terrorists are boring. Always the same serious, doom and gloom, end-of-the-world bullshit. Don't you people ever crack a joke?"

Hesbani started to squeeze the trigger. Sarah adjusted her

aim at Aziza. “Don’t do something you’ll regret, Hesbani. You pull your trigger, I pull mine.”

Hesbani released the pressure on his trigger, but seemed no less angry. His upper lip curled. “Allah’s influence has turned your people against you. Jeffrey Blanchfield, Caroline Pugh. Your own citizens are realising their own wickedness and repenting. Things are changing. What I have done will matter always.”

“I remember when Madonna mattered. Things change, don’t get over-excited.”

“Your empire will crumble. Your monarch will bleed.”

“Hate to tell you, but sis dropped her rocket launcher. Your mission is FUBAR.”

“The mission has only just begun. I am just one man. Allah’s will is infinite.”

“Your dagger tattoo is backwards.” Sarah noted the henna on his exposed wrist. The truth was that she was stalling for time while she considered her next move. If she lost her aim on Aziza, Hesbani would shoot her.

Hesbani smiled. “Al-Sharir wished to die for Allah. I wish to kill for him. Only death—”

“Can ensure life. Yeah, yeah, I’ve heard it before. God, no wonder Al-Sharir kicked you loose.”

Hesbani glanced ahead for a moment and adjusted the chopper’s trajectory. Mandy was swooping in and out of view, trying to unnerve him, but when Hesbani turned back to Sarah, his expression was cold and inhuman. “Al-Sharir is a short-sighted man. He treats war like a tea party.”

“So why use his name?”

“Because his name means more than mine. The Muslim nations will rally behind Al-Sharir. He has become a false idol, but one that can be used to achieve Allah’s goals.”

"Perhaps," Sarah said, "but we have one advantage you don't."

"What is that?"

"We can change. You might hurt us, but we'll always get back on our feet and do whatever we have to do to beat you. If we can't win now, we'll learn how to win later. You're not fighting infidels. You're fighting the future, battling progress. Change frightens small men like you. I'm sorry, Hesbani, but you're going to lose. No one can stop the human race from evolving."

Aziza started for Sarah. Sarah took one look at her and shook her head. "If you want to keep the hand you have left, *sit.*"

Aziza looked to her brother, who nodded almost imperceptibly. She sat back against the wall.

"So..." Sarah said. "Where do we go from here? You shoot me, I shoot your sister. I shoot your sister, you shoot me."

Hesbani smiled. "We've been in a similar position once before; I remember. Who lives and who dies? I believe you chose yourself last time."

Sarah nodded. "I did, but that didn't work out so well for me. Maybe this time I'll try something different. And it's *Captain*, to you, dickhead."

Sarah pulled the trigger and executed Hesbani's sister.

27

PENALTIES

"Nooooo!" Hesbani screamed and let off a shot, but Sarah had leapt out of the way. Aziza clutched her chest in shock, bleeding out.

Hesbani fired, filling the cabin with ricochets. *Ping, ping, ping!* Sarah dove behind the seat and prayed for Hesbani's firearm to empty. She soon heard a familiar and reassuring sound.

Kik Kik!

Hesbani's gun ran empty, and he threw it to the ground. Sarah rose over the back of the chair and was just about to shoot when she realised she'd dropped her own weapon while diving for cover.

Hesbani glared at Sarah, but softened when he glanced at his sister. Aziza was not yet dead, and with her final breaths she spoke to her brother. "Brother, finish... our mission. I will see you... at Allah's side."

Hesbani breathed heavily as his sister died in his arms. He whispered. "Allahu Akbar."

Aziza didn't respond.

Hesbani shoved forward on the yoke. The helicopter's

nose dipped, and they picked up speed. Sarah hit the floor behind the cockpit. She cried out in pain as she realised that one of Hesbani's ricochets had lodged in her thigh, right above her old shrapnel wound. She dragged herself towards the cockpit. "Hesbani, it's... it's over. Just give up."

"Nothing is over. I wanted to kill you in Afghanistan—Al-Sharir should have let me—but this will serve a greater purpose."

Sarah realised what Hesbani was doing, and her whole body shook, despair spreading like wildfire. He was going to dive bomb the royal barge. This was the final suicide bomb, and Sarah would be part of it.

"Don't do this," Sarah pleaded. "Your mission is a lie. No god wishes for innocent blood to be spilt. Allah doesn't want this!"

Hesbani cackled. "You know nothing of Allah's will. You are a woman, a whore."

Sarah clenched her fists. The pain in her thigh disappeared for an instant as she lunged into the cockpit and rammed into Hesbani. The man was strapped into his seat, which held him in place as she straddled his lap. He was about to protest when she silenced him with a swift headbutt. He struggled to fight her off, but she had his arms pinned beneath her thighs.

"Here's your choice," Sarah snarled. "Either I snap your neck, or I gouge out your eyes. Your choice."

Hesbani glared at her. "Fuck... you... whore."

"All right, both then." Sarah drove her thumbnails into Hesbani's eyes, ignoring the sickening feeling of yielding flesh and blood vessels rupturing.

Hesbani wailed, bucking in his seat like he was having a fit. His panic made him stronger, and he freed one of his arms.

Sarah wrapped her hands around Hesbani's neck and twisted as hard as she could.

SNAP!

Hesbani went still.

Sarah sat there for a few seconds as all the pain from her past—all the regrets, death, and bloodshed—came flooding to the surface. Sarah let out a gut-wrenching scream. She screamed so madly that it felt like her insides would explode. It was only Mattock's voice coming over the radio that snapped her out of it.

"Sarah, are you there? Speak to me."

Sarah glanced out the cockpit window and saw the Thames rushing up to meet her. Directly in front of her was the royal barge.

"Shit!"

"Sarah, are you okay? What's the situation?"

Sarah grabbed the yoke and yanked it towards her. She had no idea how to pilot a helicopter, but she prayed to mother fucking Allah that she could pull it out of the nose dive it was in. The yoke resisted her, and the entire cockpit vibrated. The helicopter continued plummeting towards the water.

Sarah kept a hold of the stick as best she could. More of the horizon appeared through the cockpit window. The city of London tilted back and forth, moving around her. She closed her eyes and hoped for the best.

When Sarah opened her eyes, she saw the console fizzing and sparking. The helicopter had come out of its nosedive and levelled out, but now someone was firing at her from below.

Tatter tatter tatter.

The helicopter rocked back and forth as its interior lights flashed. The sounds of the engine grew weaker, coughing and spluttering. The steering became heavy in her hands, and she thumbed the button on her lapel radio. "Mattock. Shit, Mattock, that goddamn frigate is firing at me. I can't fly this thing, and it's falling to pieces."

"Sarah!" It was Mandy on the line. "Keep a firm but loose grip on the yoke. Let it move freely, but keep it under your control. Guide it where you want it to go."

Sarah did as she was told. "Okay. Okay, it's working. Now what?"

"Try to level off. Keep her steady and facing forward."

"Okay, I have her steady. Now what? I can't land this thing."

"No, you can't," Mandy agreed. "You've lost your landing skids, and your petrol tank is leaking. You're going to fall out of the sky."

Sarah felt her heart sink. "So what the hell do I do?"

"Jump. Get the chopper lined up to go down in the river and jump."

Sarah didn't bother responding. She knew the helicopter was falling apart, it might even explode; she had no way of knowing. There was only one way out that gave her any hope of surviving. She stumbled into the rear cabin. Her thigh bunched in pain as shock seized her muscles. Even if she survived the long drop to the water, she was sure she couldn't swim with her injuries.

But it was the only chance she had.

There was an orange life jacket stuffed beneath one seat. She put it on. The chopper was losing altitude fast, and she was confident it would end up in a clear stretch of the river. If there was going to be casualties, it would only be her. It was enough to bring her peace in her final moments.

Mandy flew the Griffin as close as he could get. Mattock was in the co-pilot seat. The two men looked over at her and saluted, as much a sign of friendship as respect. She saluted back at them, something she thought she'd never do again after leaving the army.

"We've got you, luv," came Mattock's voice across her radio. "Soon as you hit the water, I'll be down to get you. You'll get through this, Captain, I promise."

"I know I will," she said. "And it's Sarah." She wrapped her arms around herself and jumped.

28

FINAL RESULT

The slap of the river was like getting hit by God. It knocked Sarah's senses sideways and cracked her teeth together. Her body gave up, and she sank beneath the Thames. Her empty lungs yearned for oxygen, but she felt no pain, only rising pressure. As that pressure mounted, she knew there would be blessed relief to follow.

But sinking to her death couldn't be her reward after all the heartbreak in her life. She deserved better, and she would get it. She would find peace and maybe even some happiness.

Sarah flailed every limb she could, moving upwards, towards the light. There was a chance she wouldn't make it, having sunk so low, but when she broke the surface of the water, she knew that she was alive. The sounds of the city came back, wild and panicked. She gasped for air.

Soon, the Navy surrounded her in small crafts sent forth from the HMS *Britannia.* Sailors pointed rifles at her and bellowed commands that were nothing but an audible blur. In the distance, the Never Stop News helicopter sank beneath the river, its tail boom pointing up into the air. It was comforting to know that Hesbani would sink along with it.

Sarah flinched as something hit the water beside her. At first, she thought she was being shot at again, but she turned to see it was the bottom rungs of a rope ladder.

"Told you we'd get you," Mattock shouted from the hovering Griffin.

Sarah grabbed hold of the ladder. This time she didn't mind being rescued. In fact, if Mattock wanted to carry her in his arms all the way home, that would be just fine.

Mandy hovered so close to the water that it was easy for Sarah to drag herself up. Mattock helped her climb the last few rungs before easing her into one of the seats inside the cabin. "That was one hell of an ending," he said to her. "They should make a movie about this."

Sarah sighed. "Long as I don't have to play myself, they can do whatever the hell they like."

And then there was nothing but darkness.

Sarah woke two days later in the Earthworm's infirmary—Dr Bennett leaning over her attentively. "You had quite a week, sweetheart. You've been out like a light for a while now. How're y'all feeling?"

Sarah stretched and felt pain all over her body. Her thigh was burning, and her ribs felt bruised. "I feel like I went a few rounds with a rhino," she said, "but you should see the rhino."

Sarah then fell asleep again for a few hours.

Later, she got herself up and onto a pair of crutches. The slug in her thigh hadn't gone deep, but the pain was ever-present. Palu asked her to stay, told her that MCU had been granted additional funding after its recent success. The Earthworm would be buzzing again soon, he said, delighted and more dedicated than ever.

It was then that Sarah knew Howard, Palu, Mattock, and Bennett would forever be working to protect the country against a threat that would never cease. This work was their life, and all they had was each other. Sarah might have been able to get on board with them if the scars of the past weren't so heavy on her heart. Stopping Hesbani had put a lot of her regrets to bed, but she still had a long way to go. Until she was happy with herself again, she needed to be alone. She needed to find out who the hell she was before she could even think about her future. Until she knew herself better, she couldn't afford to let people rely on her.

"You sure you won't stay?" Howard asked her as she headed up top where Mandy was waiting to take her home.

"I'm sure I can't stay," she told Howard. "But it was good meeting you. I had fun."

Howard smirked. "Fun isn't the word I'd use."

"I jumped out of a helicopter... twice. If I didn't call it fun, I'd have to call it lunacy."

"Fun it is then. I'll miss you, Sarah. Your bite's not as bad as your bark... once I got to know you."

"Tell that to Hesbani," she said, smiling. "See you, Howard. Take care of yourself."

"You too, Sarah. Stay in touch."

"Maybe."

Then Sarah had left the Earthworm forever. Mandy had taken her to her flat in Mosely, not saying a word the whole way. It wasn't awkward though. Mandy didn't get things done with words; he got things done with actions.

It had now been a week since the last attack, and the country was slipping out of panic and into outrage. The hostilities in the Middle East were going to intensify. The Americans were back onboard, and it looked like Afghanistan would be occupied for another ten years. The Taliban had been reinvigorated by Hesbani's actions, and the entire terrorist community had rallied behind the misused name of Al-Sharir. The man himself had not yet emerged to shed light on the truth. For all anyone knew, Hesbani may have killed his old mentor before any of this even began. There was trouble ahead, for sure, but Sarah wasn't the one to deal with it. Her only obligation was what she was doing right now.

Sarah kept to the periphery of Bradley's funeral. She sat at the back of the church and watched as his family and friends grieved. They shared stories about a boy who always had a kind word to say, and a young man who wanted to change the world. Sarah couldn't help but shed a tear from the tear duct that still worked.

By the time Bradley's casket was laid into the earth, Sarah felt more in touch with herself than she had since she'd felt a baby growing inside her. She owed it to Bradley to show kindness wherever she could. The world had been deprived of someone wonderful, and she had to fill that void as much as she could. She would no doubt come up short, but she would do her best.

Sarah edged behind a willow tree as the funeral wrapped up. Howard, Palu, Mattock, and Bennett were there, but they hadn't spotted her. Their grief was deep and real, their focus entirely on Bradley. That was the way Sarah wanted it. She needed to put the past behind her, and holding a reunion was not conducive to that.

It was time to go. She said her goodbyes and said a quick prayer. Bradley was gone, and now she needed to leave too. She stepped backwards, remaining concealed behind the willow tree. There was a bus stop nearby that would take her home.

Sarah headed for the gateway to the churchyard. She walked backwards, not wanting to look away until she had to. There was a part of her that wanted to run up to Bradley's grieving family and tell them what a brave hero he'd been, but she knew that wasn't the right thing to do. She needed to turn around and walk away. She had to face the future.

But something was tugging at her. The future was right in front of her, but she still wanted to run away from it. After what she had been through with the members of MCU, it almost felt like she'd been part of a family again. Despite the horror of everything she'd been through, the gaping hole inside of her had felt a little fuller.

"What am I doing?" she asked herself. "I have a chance to do something with my life. There's a place for me, and I'm running away."

Sarah knew what she had to do. It was time to put the fear and pain behind her and finally take a chance on something. She belonged with MCU.

Sarah spun around, ready to head back to the funeral and ask Palu and the others for a second chance, but when she turned, she bumped into someone standing in her way.

Her eyes went wide. "You!"

"Yes... me."

Sarah's world went dark as a thick bag was shoved over her head, and something hard struck the base of her skull. She tried to call out for her friends, but as she faded, she realised she had none

Continue Sarah's story in book 2: HOT ZONE

WANT FREE BOOKS?

Don't miss out on your FREE Iain Rob Wright horror starter pack. Five free bestselling horror novels sent straight to your inbox. No strings attached.

For more information just visit this page:
www.iainrobwright.com

PLEA FROM THE AUTHOR

Hey, Reader. So you got to the end of my book. I hope that means you enjoyed it. Whether or not you did, I would just like to thank you for giving me your valuable time to try and entertain you. I am truly blessed to have such a fulfilling job, but I only have that job because of people like you; people kind enough to give my books a chance and spend their hard-earned money buying them. For that I am eternally grateful.

If you would like to find out more about my other books then please visit my website for full details. You can find it at:

http://www.iainrobwright.com.

Also feel free to contact me on Facebook, Twitter, or email (all details on the website), as I would love to hear from you.

If you enjoyed this book and would like to help, then you could think about leaving a review on Amazon, Goodreads, or anywhere else that readers visit. The most important part of how well a book sells is how many positive reviews it has, so if you leave me one then you are directly helping me to continue on this journey as a fulltime writer. Thanks in advance to anyone who does. It means a lot.

More books available from Iain Rob Wright

Sarah Stone Thriller Series

- Soft Target
- Hot Zone
- End Play

Other books

- Animal Kingdom
- AZ of Horror
- 2389
- Holes in the Ground (with J.A.Konrath)
- Sam
- ASBO
- The Final Winter
- The Housemates
- Sea Sick
- Ravage
- Savage
- The Picture Frame
- Wings of Sorrow
- The Gates
- Legion
- Extinction
- TAR
- House Beneath the Bridge
- The Peeling

- Dark Ride
- Escape!

Iain Rob Wright is one of the UK's most successful horror and suspense writers, with novels including the critically acclaimed, THE FINAL WINTER; the disturbing bestseller, ASBO; and the wicked screamfest, THE HOUSEMATES.

His work is currently being adapted for graphic novels, audio books, and foreign audiences. He is an active member of the Horror Writer Association and a massive animal lover.

www.iainrobwright.com
FEAR ON EVERY PAGE

For more information
www.iainrobwright.com
iain.robert.wright@hotmail.co.uk

Artwork by Stuart Bache at Books Covered Ltd

Images provided by Shutterstock

Printed in Great Britain
by Amazon

66037496R00163